The Voyage of Sam Singh

ALSO BY GITA RALLEIGH

The Destiny of Minou Moonshine

The Voyage of Sam Singh

GITA RALLEIGH

ZEPHYR

An imprint of Head of Zeus

This is a Zephyr book first published in the UK in 2024 by
Head of Zeus, part of Bloomsbury Publishing Plc.

9 7 5 3 1 2 4 6 8

A catalogue record for this book is available from the British Library.

PBO: 9781804545522
E: 9781804545492

Cover: Weitong Mai

Printed and bound in Great Britain by
CPI Group (UK) Ltd, Croydon CR0 4YY

Head of Zeus Ltd
First Floor East
5–8 Hardwick Street
London ECIR 4RG
www.headofzeus.com

For Akira, Taro & Keita

One

S am felt the sharp dig of claws almost tug the hair from his scalp, startling him awake. '*Ow!* Suka – that hurt!'

With a flurry of emerald wings, the parrot settled on his chest, tilting his head hopefully. '*Breakfast, Sam Singh!*'

Sam yawned, blinked at the glare of daylight and reached to scratch the bird's rosy neck. The uneasy sway of the ship's deck had made him horribly seasick last night and he felt too queasy for food. 'Is it morning already? I don't have anything for you to eat, Suka – hang on!' He delved into his pocket and found an old bag of peanuts. 'How about these?'

'*Peanuts! Monkey nuts! Cacahuetes!*'

'*Kadalai, mungfali!* Good boy! We're due at the port today. Let's see if we can spot land.'

Sam clambered up the ladder on to the bridge of the steamship. The funnel billowed sooty smoke into the sky, streaked pink with dawn. Below, the *Yellow Pearl*'s foredeck thronged with passengers eager to disembark. Tradesmen with bundles of goods huddled close to the stack, white-uniformed sailors stood between them and the first-class passengers at the ship's prow, who gripped their straw hats as the wind tugged at the brims. Stewards weaved through the crowd, carrying luggage from cabins.

'*Land ahoy! Kinara dekho!*' screeched Suka joyfully, swooping over turquoise water.

In the distance, the turtle-shaped outline of the Isle of Lost Voices emerged from milky sea mist. Sam leaned forward, taking deep breaths of briny air as the Isle grew closer. His eyes roamed its green hills, silver sand and jagged cliffs of rock, unsure of what he was looking for. And then he saw it – a tower made from the Isle's black stone, and polished so that it glittered darkly in the sun.

'The Octopus, Suka!' Sam whispered, as the parrot landed on his shoulder.

His stomach lurched wildly as he stared at the building, hulking over the curve of the bay. 'That's where Moon's locked up. I'm sure of it.'

Moon was Sam's older brother. Their father had died when Sam was small, and Moon provided for the family. Like all land pirates, he could swarm over roofs, scale walls like a monkey and contort himself through the tiniest spaces. Moon had wriggled his way out of every jail, lock-up or police station he'd been held in. Until three years ago, when he'd left on a job and not come home. The police jeered at Sam's widowed mother when she reported his brother missing. He was not popular with the authorities.

Whenever Moon planned a job, he'd say to Sam, *What's the worst that could happen, eh Sam? Transportation!* Sam knew what transportation meant. It meant being shipped to the Isle and its notorious Octopus prison, never to return to the mainland.

'Hey! Boy with the parrot,' a steward called. 'Fetch the professor's trunks. You're not paid to stand around sunning yourself!'

'Yes, sir,' Sam saluted smartly.

A professor – known to Sam's people as the Collector – had paid his passage on the *Yellow Pearl*. The Collector travelled the world, gathering languages. Sam, like Suka, spoke five and had translated the land pirates' lingo for him. When the Collector needed a servant for his trip to the Isle,

Sam offered himself for hire. His mother wasn't happy, but with money tight, Sam's new stepfather had agreed at once.

'Do that boy good to earn for a change,' he'd sneered. 'Twelve years old, he's too big to be in school. And you –' he'd given Sam a cuff on the ear – 'come straight back with the cash – no running off like your feckless brother!'

Sam had kept his mouth shut and nodded, remembering Moon's words.

What's the worst that could happen, eh, Sam? Transportation!

Moon was the reason Sam had taken the Collector's job and with it, free passage across the Kalinga Sea to the Isle of Lost Voices.

Sam leaped over the railing to a warning shout from one of the lascars and neatly dodged the crane's huge rope, uncoiling to unload the ship's cargo. Threading his way nimbly through piles of mailsacks and travelling cases, he hurried below deck. The professor's cabin door was open and he staggered back up the steps with the man's heavy trunks, groaning as he set them down. What did the professor have in them? Sam only carried the clothes on his back and a packet of peanuts his mother had given him – Suka had eaten most of those. Stacking the trunks on the foredeck, he moved to the guard rail, Suka perched beside him, to take in the view of the Isle as they drew into harbour.

The Octopus prison reared from the clifftop, overshadowing the port's huddle of brick warehouses, wooden huts and fishing boats. The domed black tower was studded by round windows, reflecting pale sky. Eight wings snaked from it like dark tentacles, giving the place a monstrous look that made Sam shiver, despite the warm sunshine.

'*Collector! Sam! The Collector!*' Suka had soared from his perch to circle above the passengers' heads.

Sam scanned the crowd and spotted the tall man in his khaki safari suit and helmet at the prow. He ducked quickly from the rail to guard the luggage. Sam did not plan to stick with the Collector for long. Once on the Isle, he'd slip away and find work. Then, he'd be free to do what he'd really come for: find his brother.

He glanced down at the scorpion tattooed on his arm, a mark that identified the boys and men of his tribe, dead or alive.

We are kings of the forest.
Let them tame us if they can!

Moon had taught him those words: the land pirates' greeting. Sam missed his brother terribly.

Life was hard without him, especially with his new stepfather around. Sam's mother had remarried after Moon's disappearance. He now had a little sister who was sweet, if noisy and sticky-faced. He was less fond of his stepfather, who drank too much; any money he earned soon vanished into the bottle. Moon had kept Sam from the life of a land pirate but to his stepfather, Sam was just another mouth to feed. Whatever anyone said, he knew his brother would never run off and abandon him.

Which meant the worst had happened. *Transportation.* And if Moon really was locked up in the Octopus, Sam did not intend to leave the Isle without him.

Two

'Parrot boy! Where have you been?' Sam jumped at the booming voice of the Collector. 'Lie that big case flat! Those are fragile specimens.'

Sam rearranged the cases with a sigh. Suka swooped to his shoulder as the man approached.

'Well, that's the first work I've seen since we boarded. I know your people are work shy, but I'm not having this!' The Collector did not sound happy.

Sam looked at his feet and tried to appear sorry. Maybe he'd get the sack, leaving him free to look for Moon.

'*Seasick!*' Suka screeched unhelpfully. '*Sam Singh, seasick! Beemar! Malade!*'

An elegant young woman in a white lace sari turned to look at Sam as she passed by. She frowned at the Collector, her eyes masked by a huge pair of glasses.

'Professor Bogusz, surely you wouldn't dismiss this boy if he was seasick?' she said sharply. 'How old is he, anyway? Have you had breakfast, Sam Singh?'

Sam shook his head. 'I haven't eaten since we left Indica,' he said truthfully, his stomach growling to back him up.

The Collector flushed. 'Naturally I would not, Princess. He's all right, aren't you, boy? Tough people, his tribe of land pirates. Hunters, craftsmen and petty thieves, but spirited with it.'

The princess smiled at Sam. 'And who is this remarkable parrot?'

'*Suka! Suka!*' the bird shrieked in answer.

'Suka! How wonderful. Well, I must be off, Sam. Perhaps we'll meet again on the Isle?'

Sam watched the passengers shuffle and part to make way for the princess, who glided across the gangway ahead of the crowd. She was followed by a porter carrying her bags and a young man in a yellow turban, whistling.

He looked again and rubbed his eyes. Last night, shivering and retching, while half-asleep on deck, he'd heard a voice say, 'By the Lady – you're in a bad way! Drink this.'

Sam was so thirsty, he'd drunk the cool lemony water in one long gulp and fallen into a deep sleep. He remembered now. In the blue moonlight, all he'd seen of his helper was a yellow turban and the glint of a diamond earring. The fellow who'd cured his seasickness was the princess's servant!

The Collector turned to another of the first-class passengers. 'Not what I'd call a *real* princess. They're hardly proper royalty – she's from one of those tiny states. Moonlally, I think it's called.'

Sam stared after the princess at the mention of Moonlally. Land pirates named their children for the city where they were born. Moonlally was his brother Moon's real name, just as Samudra, the great city on the Indican Ocean, was Sam's. The princess meant well, but hadn't done him a favour by intervening with the Collector. Now Sam would have to find the right moment to slip away.

'She's visiting the Isle to inspect the prison,' the Collector droned on. 'We struck up quite an acquaintance – very young, of course, but not unintelligent. I told her of my theories on—' The ship's foghorn blared out, drowning the rest of his words.

Sam brightened. If the princess was visiting the jail, he could ask the servant in the yellow turban to help him find Moon.

As the sound of the horn faded, the Collector looked round to see the other passenger edging away.

'Know what that big black building is, boy?' he barked.

Sam nodded. 'A jail, sir – they call it the Octopus.'

'Of course! I'll wager some of your lot are inside. They don't call you land pirates for nothing – wily bunch of thieves and scoundrels.'

Sam jumped. 'Er, I don't know of anyone, sir.' He touched the inked scorpion on his arm, hoping the Collector hadn't seen his reaction.

Sam knew Moon wouldn't have done anything too awful. Land pirates were honourable thieves who took only what they needed and robbed from those too rich to notice. But he wasn't silly enough to tell the Collector – outsiders had their own opinions of right and wrong. Besides, Moon had wanted more for Sam. He'd taken all the risks of land-pirate ways so his younger brother could stay in school.

'The interior of the Isle is where we're heading: dense, impenetrable jungle,' the Collector continued. 'The governor has arranged for the forest people to guide us – if they turn up. Their tribe's as unreliable as you land pirates, I hear.

Now, take the luggage to his car – I'm staying at the Residence tonight.'

'Yes, sir,' Sam saluted. He lugged the Collector's trunks down the gangway, wishing he could carry them on his head, like the porters jostling for business. Sam was sure he'd learn to balance stacks of luggage as easily as they did – the port would be a good place to find work while he schemed his way into the Octopus.

Passengers poured down the gangway from the steamer as the crane swung back and forth, unloading its cargo: crates of spices, tea and grain, which spilled on to the dock. Sam spotted the Collector's pith helmet beside the gleaming black motor car belonging to the governor.

He loaded the cases into the trunk and hesitated, before climbing up on the running board of the car. If he was going to run, he ought to run now. But he was faint with hunger, his stomach rumbling loudly over the sound of the engine. The Collector hadn't paid him, he didn't have another job – and there wouldn't be easy pickings at the port, too many uniforms. He'd be wiser to sneak away tonight, after a decent meal.

The car trundled off. Suka flew above as they jolted slowly along the dusty road, lined with windblown palm trees. Hearing shouts, Sam looked back at the dock. Flanked by their guards, a line of downcast prisoners in black trudged from the *Yellow Pearl*, chains clanking. Sam couldn't tear his eyes away until they'd rounded the corner and the men were out of sight. He was gripped by fear as he pictured Moon among them – shackled in the hold for the desperate, rolling sea voyage and reaching land, to be locked in that horrible jail. Shuddering, he turned to face the road that unfurled ahead, hoping – believing – it might lead him to his brother.

Three

It was a short journey to the Governor's Residence – the largest house and almost the largest building Sam had ever seen. It was painted white, with a green-tiled roof, rising three storeys high. Sam started counting the windows, but soon gave up – they went on for ever. A whole town could live in that house, never mind his own tribe.

The governor's car swept around the front lawn, with its marble statue of a man on horseback at the centre. When it halted at the wide mahogany doors, Sam was glad he didn't have to go inside. Instead, a housekeeper, a plump lady in a pristine uniform, came to whisk him round the back.

'I suppose you're hungry?' she said, looking him up and down. 'Boys always are. Let's get you fed.'

'Thank you – I was seasick, so I didn't eat on board. Can I help out in return?' Sam asked. 'Any odd jobs you need doing?'

The housekeeper, whose name was Bela, smiled. 'You've not stayed in a big house before, have you, son? The Residence has an army of staff – I have three girls polishing floors alone. And you look green as a ghost. I'll fetch you a plate from the kitchen – you can take it into the gardens to eat.'

This suited Sam. Before he did anything, he needed food and a night's rest. Tomorrow, the Collector would travel to meet the Isle's original people and record their language. He knew the governor had arranged a guide from the forest dwellers to lead him – he'd have no need of Sam.

Sam carried his supper of bread, cheese and mango pickle out to the grounds of the Residence. Rolling lawns stretched towards a body of water glinting in the moonlight. On either side stood shadowy groves of trees and long paths edged with flowering shrubs. Suka snaffled a crust and flitted off to explore. Sam hoped he would return soon. He was used to sleeping outdoors, but the gardens felt too quiet without his tribe around him. Curling up under a shady tree, the air heavy with the scent of jasmine, he soon fell into a deep and dreamless sleep.

In the night, Sam was woken by a clatter of echoing horse's hooves. It was still pitch-black, the moon high. Strangely, he hadn't heard voices to suggest another guest had arrived. He yawned loudly, too tired to puzzle it over. Suka fluttered down from his perch in the branches above.

'*Sam Singh?*'

'Go back to sleep, boy. Wake me at day break?'

He was awoken later by the parrot squawking, '*Stranger! Anniyan! Ajnabi!*'

Sam sat up. It was barely light, the low sun still red over the distant horizon.

'What stranger? There's no one here, Suka!' he groaned. 'Anyway, we're up. Let's run before the Collector's awake. The guide won't be here yet – he said those forest people are unreliable – *ouch!*' He felt a sharp pain sting his cheek, as if someone had thrown a tiny stone.

'*Étranger, Sam!*' Suka called again, fluttering down from the tree in agitation. '*Stranger!*'

Sam squinted curiously into the spreading branches of the red-flowering paulownia. A round-faced, curly-haired girl in a faded dress was glaring at him through its glossy leaves. She was holding a long bamboo tube.

'Hey – that hurt!' he yelled.

She slid down the trunk and faced him. 'You're

lucky I didn't hit that bird of yours with my blowpipe. How did you teach a pet parrot to speak?'

Sam shrugged, not wanting a conversation with someone who'd just attacked him. Wiping away a trickle of blood, he scrambled up and whistled for Suka, who flew to perch on his shoulder. But when he turned away, the girl was standing in front of him. She had strung the paulownia's red flowers into a garland, which she wore around her neck.

'You're not sulking about that tiny scratch? It's only a bamboo stick and dried berries. I can teach you how to make one. If you show me how to trap my own pet parrot…'

'I didn't trap Suka!' Sam reached up to ruffle the parrot's feathers. 'He fell from the nest when he was a fledgling, didn't you, boy? I raised him but he's not a pet, he's my friend. Anyway, I have to go now.'

'Go where? Don't you work for that professor? What's he like?'

'What's it got to do with you?'

The girl clicked her teeth, impatiently. 'I'm the guide, stupid. One of those *unreliable* forest people.' She thrust her hand towards Sam. 'Call me Lola.'

Sam, cheek still throbbing, shook Lola's hand warily. 'I'm Sam Singh,' he muttered. 'Was that your horse I heard arriving last night?'

'Stupid! Where would I get a horse? I walked here. That was old Colonel Mayonnaise.'

'Mayonnaise?'

The girl looked at him. '*Colonel* Mayonnaise,' she said slowly, as if talking to a small child. 'First ruler of the Isle. His statue's out front. Didn't you see it?'

'What about it?'

'He – *it* – comes alive. Gallops round the Residence at midnight,' Lola said matter-of-factly. 'Don't you know anything about the Isle of Lost Voices? Plenty of ghosts, especially at the port. Clanking chains, howls, screams, the lot.'

Sam shot her a worried glance. He'd come to find out whether Moon was in prison – but did he really want to work at the port if it was haunted by ghosts?

'Anyhow, parrot boy. Time for breakfast!' Lola strolled past him, heading towards the kitchens.

'*Breakfast!*' Suka squawked happily. '*Nashtha, petit déjeuner, kaalai unavu.*'

'Nado – that's what we call it,' Lola called behind her.

'*Nado! Nado, nado,*' Suka repeated.

Lola laughed. 'You don't have to teach that clever bird! He picks it up himself. Come on!'

Sam paused to pull on his sandals before following her across the lawn. The dew-soaked grass was as tempting to walk on as any carpet, but Sam was always alert for snakes. She led him past a grove of mango and calabash trees, pale orchids hanging from their branches.

'Do you live at the Residence?' he asked. Lola seemed to know her way around.

She shook her head. 'I only visit when the governor needs an interpreter. I live in our village, with my grandfather. This way!'

She unlatched the back door to the kitchen and propped it open with a brick. Steamy air escaped, carrying the smell of baking bread, frying sausages and other good things. Sam knew he needed to shake Lola off to slip away, but recovering from seasickness had left him ravenous. Breakfast was far too delicious to pass up.

Four

'Joseph!' Lola called to the cook, a large man dressed in white who flapped a dishcloth at her. 'Can we get breakfast? Me and parrot boy are starving!'

'Not *now*, Lola. I'm busy!'

'Just coffee and bread rolls? Maybe those seeded ones, for the parrot!' Lola wheedled. 'And a sausage or two?'

Joseph sighed. 'Go on. Take them and get out. The governor has an important guest for lunch – the Princess of Moonlally, would you believe! He's asked for a suckling pig, candied ginger and fruit jellies. Where am I meant to find luxuries on this godforsaken isle, tell me?'

'I'd have got you a wild pig, if you'd asked,' Lola told him cheerfully, balancing a jug of coffee, a plate of sausages and a bread basket on a tray. 'Nabbed a fine one the other day. Sam – cups!'

Sam picked up a couple of tin mugs from the sink, and they headed back out to the lawns. He polished off two sausages and a bread roll, feeding Suka the seeds, while he thought over his plans. If the Princess of Moonlally was a guest at lunch, he could track down her servant in the yellow turban. And *he* might lead Sam to the prison and Moon.

'This is the first time I've guided a stranger to our village,' Lola mused. 'What's he like, parrot boy? Your Professor *Bogusz*.'

'My name's Sam. It's not hard to say,' he pointed out huffily. 'We call him the Collector because he wanders round collecting languages. He came to write down our people's tongue.'

'Strange. What is a *professor* anyway?'

'A schoolteacher for grown-ups.'

Lola scoffed. 'Grown-ups don't go to school! Do you, Sam?'

He nodded. 'We travel about, but my brother still made me go. I didn't mind it.' Apart from the other children, who were rude about land pirates and refused to let him join in their games.

'I hated school,' Lola told him. 'The governor hired a tutor for me instead. He used to climb into the tree for our lessons. Anyway, once you learn to read, you can teach yourself the rest. The governor lets me borrow any books I want from his library.'

Sam smiled. He was beginning to like Lola. He decided the best plan would be to stay at the Residence and offer help. With any luck, he'd catch the yellow-turbaned servant passing through.

But later that day, as he scrubbed dishes, the housekeeper came bustling in.

'The governor's asking for parrot boy!' she told him. 'Lola too – goodness knows where she's got to. Probably up a tree somewhere.'

'I'll call her, if you like?' Sam offered, wiping his hands on his shirt. This was his chance! If the princess was at lunch, her servant had to be close by.

'Quick, then, run and fetch her!' the housekeeper told him, hurrying off. 'Lola knows the way to the dining room.'

'What do they want us for?' Lola called down from the branches of the paulownia.

Sam shielded his eyes from the sun. 'Bela didn't say.'

She slid down the trunk in one swift movement. 'I suppose we'd better go if the governor's called us. We might get leftovers from the royal luncheon.'

Sam followed her to another entrance, where she slipped off her sandals. Glass shelves lined the hallway, filled with fragile-looking statues, vases and china plates. Sam practically tiptoed, terrified he'd break something. Lola scampered over the polished floors and silk rugs in her bare and none too clean feet, stopping to point out a huge painting that took up most of one wall.

'That's old Mayo!' she said conversationally. 'He's not so bad – for a ghost.'

Sam stared at the portrait of a man in a gold-buttoned red coat and wig, sitting on a padded throne. His eyes seemed to follow them as Lola rapped on the double doors to the dining room and pushed them open.

'Lola, dear!' The governor, a broad red-faced man, called. 'Come in!' he added to Sam, who halted at the doorway. 'We don't bite. Where's this parrot I've heard about?'

'Er – in the gardens, sir.' Sam almost didn't recognise the Collector, who wore a black dinner jacket in place of his safari suit and helmet. He came towards them, taking an instrument out of a wooden box. Sam took a step backwards.

'Line up, children. Professor Bogusz and I have

laid on a sporting bet,' the governor bellowed. 'I'm betting on you, Lola dear. Cleverest young lady on the Isle.'

Lola and Sam exchanged mystified glances. Sam was a few centimetres or so shorter than Lola, but the Collector didn't seem interested in how tall they were. He muttered to himself as he – there was no other word for it – *measured* Sam's head, front to back and side to side. The measuring instrument had two curved claws that clicked into place, attached to a metal slide. Sam didn't understand what it was all about.

'Well!' the governor called. 'What do those callipers tell you? Professor Bogusz,' he addressed the table, 'claims he can predict who might commit crime from the shape of the skull in childhood. Save us building jails, what?'

Sam lowered his eyes from the stares of those around the table, feeling heat and shame flood his face. He looked down at the patterned carpet. Could the Collector really tell he was a land pirate just by the shape of his head? And what did that have to do with Lola?

The Collector's claws now pincered Lola's head. Sam glanced up at the guests, who had returned to eating their lunch – except the princess, who met his gaze. She looked horrified.

'What are you *doing*, Professor?' she cried.

'Measuring the skull's dimensions. It doesn't hurt!'

'Ow! It does, actually.' Lola scowled at the Collector as if she might punch him. Sam wished she would.

'Lola, keep still, dear, he's almost finished. Tell us, how do those numbers help you, Bogusz?' the governor asked, leaning towards them.

The Collector released the claws and scribbled numbers into a small notebook. He cleared his throat. 'Well, those with criminal tendencies have certain characteristics: a small vault, the low brow and so on.'

He glanced at Sam and Lola, dismissing them with a wave of his hand. 'Off you go – back to the kitchens.' Lola turned on her heel and flounced. Sam attempted an awkward bow, then backed out of the room, closing the doors softly, the word *criminal* still ringing in his ears.

Five

Back in the bustle of the kitchens, Lola gave Sam a puzzled look.

'What was all *that* about? she asked, picking up a pair of kitchen tongs. 'I'm the Collec-*tor*. Here, Joseph, let me measure your head for criminal tender-seas,' she mimicked, waving them in the air.

'Put those down!' the cook fumed. 'And scarper, both of you, or you'll get no leftover roast pork from me – not a scrap.'

Lola dropped the tongs into the sink and ran off to the gardens, laughing. Sam followed, hearing Suka squawking his name as he neared the big paulownia. '*Sam Singh!*'

A young man in a yellow turban was feeding Suka sunflower seeds under the tree.

'Who's *that*?' Lola stopped.

'It's you – from the *Yellow Pearl*!' Sam exclaimed, thrilled to have caught the princess's servant. 'Sorry, I never caught your name. I wanted to thank you – for curing my seasickness.'

The young man grinned. In daylight he was even younger than Sam remembered – without his moustache, he might have been Moon's age.

'Call me Sparrow,' he said, shaking Sam's hand. 'Suka's already told me you're Sam Singh – looking a lot healthier than last time we met! And you are…?' he asked, turning to bow to Lola.

'This is Lola,' Sam told him. 'Lola, meet Sparrow. He's with the—'

'*More* strangers?' Lola frowned. 'Why are you all here?'

'I'm with the Princess of Moonlally, inspecting the jail. We're investigating reports they treat prisoners terribly out here. Shackles, isolation, forced labour…'

Lola scowled. 'We don't like strangers on the Isle! My people managed without jails – or roads or electric light – before you came along. Come on, Suka!' She whistled to the parrot, who fluttered to her shoulder. 'I'll be up there if you want me, Sam.' She darted away towards a grove of trees at the far end of the gardens.

Sam smiled apologetically. 'Lola doesn't like new people. She hit me with a blowpipe this morning.' He winced as he touched the cut on his cheek.

Sparrow gave a sympathetic nod. 'I can understand why she—'

'You're from Moonlally!' Sam broke in. 'That's my brother's name. In our tribe, we're called after the place we're born, see – I'm Sam, short for Samudra.' He hoped Sparrow would ask after Moon, giving him the chance to seek help.

'Samudra Singh. That's a fine name!' Sparrow grinned. 'How did you fall in with Professor Bogusz? That man has peculiar ideas.'

Sam nodded and rubbed his temples, still feeling the tight grip of callipers. 'He came to write down my tribe's language and took a liking to Suka – said he'd never known such a clever parrot. He offered me a job. I carry stuff, wash clothes, make tea. It's not hard. Except for lugging his big case of specimens around. That's tricky, because they're fragile.'

'Specimens?' Sparrow raised an eyebrow. 'What sort of specimens does a professor of anthropology collect?'

He shrugged. 'Not sure, exactly. I've never seen inside.'

'You're trekking inland with the professor and Lola, I suppose?'

Sam flinched, avoiding answering directly. 'Yes, er, Lola's the guide. She's all right, once she gets to know you.'

'Most people are, Sam Singh.' Sparrow smiled, then turned at the sound of Bela the housekeeper's voice. 'Ah – I'm being summoned to drive the princess home. Good to meet you.'

'But wait – there was something I wanted to ask. About the prison, and my brother, Moon—'

'Come and see us!' Sparrow called back. 'The princess would be delighted. We're staying in the old bungalow, halfway up the hill – until the *Yellow Pearl* sails again!'

That night, Sam lay awake. Suka was perched above him in the paulownia tree, while Lola slept in a hammock strung between its branches. He ought to run and escape the Collector while he had the chance but whenever he tried to move, his skin grew clammy and his limbs froze at the eerie clip-clopping of hooves. General Mayonnaise's statue had rounded the Residence three times and Sam didn't dare leave during its ghostly night-time gallop. At least he knew Sparrow and the princess were on the Isle until the *Yellow Pearl* sailed. Once daylight came, he would make his way up the hill to find them.

He remembered what Sparrow said about the Collector's big case marked: *FRAGILE*. Sam was curious about what was inside too. What kind of specimens would the Collector be so interested in?

The following morning came Sam's chance to find out. He was sent for by the Collector, who planned to leave the large trunk in one of the Residence's outbuildings while they trekked inland. The outbuilding – the Collector called it a *folly* – stood on an island in the centre of an ornamental lake.

'Careful now. Any breakages come off your wages,' the man warned, as Sam heaved the huge case on to a wide wooden boat. He rowed them across, then hitched the boat securely to its post and lugged the case into the octagonal wooden folly, which had windows hung with cane blinds.

'Place my specimens in the centre of the room. They'll be safe and dry here,' the Collector told him, pulling a bunch of keys from his jacket. 'I must check they haven't been damaged.'

Sam hardly dared breathe as he watched the man unfasten the padlock and lift the padded lid of the case. Light spilled over rows of domed, bone-coloured objects. Was he collecting the eggs of some giant bird?

The Collector looked up at Sam and cleared his throat. 'Wait in the boat, boy.'

Sam nodded. 'I'll raise the blinds to let more daylight in for you, sir.'

Whistling loudly, he walked towards the boat. Then, silent as any land pirate, Sam sneaked back to the folly. He cleaned a corner of the window with his sleeve and peered through the glass. The Collector lifted one of the domed objects up to the light and turned it slowly. He paused to blow off the gathered dust. Sam swallowed, revulsion rising in his throat, as he saw they were not bone-coloured eggs, but *actual bones*.

The Collector's case was neatly packed with row upon row of human skulls, a number in black ink scrawled upon each ivory vault.

Six

Sam's arms trembled as he rowed the Collector back across the lake. He followed him through the grounds at a distance, trying to make sense of all he'd seen. The Collector had told lies, or half-truths. He didn't only collect words, but *people* – what was left of them, anyway. How did human skulls help him understand the language of the land pirates, or of Lola's tribe?

He wanted to run more than ever, but the governor's car awaited them, travel packs loaded. Lola, sandals strung around her neck, was hopping impatiently from one bare foot to another.

'There you are, Sam Singh!' she called. 'Come on – I can't wait to show you our village.'

Not knowing what to do, he climbed on to the running board and rubbed his eyes, trying to erase the vision of those skulls, packed neatly into the Collector's padded case.

'Are you all right, Sam?' Lola asked over the purr of the engine. 'Your face is a funny colour – green, nearly. There's nothing to be scared of.'

'Why would I be scared?' Sam blinked.

'I expect they told you about the salties on the Isle?' Lola called as the car rumbled off. 'Saltwater crocodiles – the meanest kind. I won't let them eat you, city boy!'

Sam didn't answer. He wasn't a city boy, and had seen plenty of crocs – freshwater rather than salt, but they couldn't be *that* different.

'*Sam Singh sad!*' Suka cried as he flew above them. '*Il est triste! Dukh! Varuttam!*'

Suka always knew when he was upset. But he wasn't sad, only disturbed. He wondered what the measurements made of him and Lola had to do with what he'd witnessed.

'I expect you're missing home, Sam,' Lola said gently.

He sighed. 'I'm fine.'

Lola was wrong. There was nothing left for him at home, not any more. As the car trundled round the turns, Sam glimpsed the Octopus's domed tower. Was his brother inside its tentacled cells, now skulking behind the buildings of the port?

And was he, Sam, doomed to end up in prison like Moon? Small and wiry in build, he knew the land pirates had uses for boys like him.

Sam remembered the Collector's words: *criminal tendencies*, and felt a flush of shame. But he knew the man's ideas were rubbish. For a start, the Collector, with his big head, only spoke one language, while Suka the parrot spoke five.

His heart lifted as the car climbed the hills, leaving the bustle and noise of the port behind. The road grew narrow as they travelled inland, tarmac giving way to packed dirt and then to a muddy, twisting track cutting through lush, forested slopes. They were driving towards the largest river on the Isle, which they would journey up in a canoe to reach Lola's village.

Finally, the car pulled up at a wooden pier, jutting over a broad, rushing river. Two men stood there, who looked like Lola, with her dark, gleaming skin and clouds of curly hair. Their faces were decorated with intricate yellow patterns of swirling circles and lines.

'There they are!' Lola whooped, leaping from the running board and darting to the end of the pier where they chattered in their own language. Suka swooped after her and perched on her shoulder.

Sam told himself he didn't mind – Suka was a friend, not a pet. He was free to fly anywhere he wanted. But he couldn't help feeling hurt at how quickly the parrot had taken to Lola.

The Collector climbed out of the car. Sam heaved the packs from the back seat on to the sandy ground. There were three, one for Sam to carry and two for the guides. The man opened one and took out a wide khaki hat with netting at the front to replace his helmet. He checked the front pockets of his safari jacket. Sam knew the right-hand one contained the Collector's notebook, where he scrawled his findings. As he opened the left-hand pocket, Sam glimpsed the metallic glint of a pistol. What did he need *that* for?

'Right! Let's be off. We will meet you here in three days,' the Collector spoke slowly to the driver, holding up three fingers. '*Three days.* Yes?'

'Very good, sir,' the driver mumbled. He slammed the car door, started the engine and sped down the road, as if he couldn't wait to escape. Sam watched him drive off and wished that he was leaving too. He felt as if he'd taken a wrong turn and was heading along an unknown path.

Hearing raised voices, he looked back to see the Collector scowling at Lola's people, who stood with their arms folded. Sam abandoned the packs

– there was no one to steal them, anyway – and walked over to see what the trouble was. He was good at breaking up fights – usually between his mother and stepfather.

'What's up?' he asked Lola.

Lola pointed at the packs. 'The Johns won't carry those heavy packs. Not unless he pays them more.'

'What else are they being paid for?' the Collector spluttered. 'Did they think I'd trek to the jungle with only the clothes on my back?'

Lola, in her red dress and sandals, shrugged and glanced pointedly at the men, who wore only a short cloth around their middle. 'They agreed a price to guide you to our village. No one said they had to carry your stuff… like a donkey!'

'*Donkey!*' crowed Suka. '*Baudet! Kaluthai! Gadha!*'

The men stared at Suka in amazement. 'Gadha!' one of them repeated. He pointed to the packs. 'Gadha!'

The word seemed to make them angrier. *Donkey* was an insult in many languages, Sam knew, though a donkey was a valued family member to the land pirates, who were always on the move. All his family's possessions would have fitted inside the Collector's three huge packs.

Both men shouted, gesturing at the Collector, whose face was now a livid red.

'What on earth are they saying?' he spat.

'Like I said, they want payment for the extra work!' Lola explained. 'What's inside those big packs, anyway?' Sam had wondered about this too.

'Supplies, girl, what else?

'You mean food?'

'Food, medicine, tobacco, a little whisky for the stomach...'

'That'll do!' Lola said promptly, and whispered to the two men, who nodded. 'They'll take the tobacco and whisky.' She smiled angelically.

The Collector's face was purple. Sam thought he might be having some kind of attack. He stepped forward to help.

'Shall I fetch those items from your pack, sir?'

The man's shoulders slumped. He looked back at the dusty track they had driven down, and at the wooden dugout canoe tied to the pier. The river was shadowed by huge trees and light through the canopy glowed green in the afternoon sun. The air hummed with insects and the cries of strange birds.

He nodded, defeated, and beckoned Sam closer. 'Give them Bengal Rum – not the Scotch,' he whispered. 'And chewing tobacco.'

Sam hurried over and found the bottle of Bangla Daru and three bright packets of cheap tobacco, which he'd seen the Collector burning to keep mosquitoes off. He strode up to Lola. 'Here you go.'

She shot him a look. 'They don't bite, you know. Not unless you give them a reason.'

Sam hadn't been nervous, only unsure of how to address the two men. He smiled, bowed for good measure (they found this amusing) and handed over the goods, which they tucked into their waistbands.

Suka plummeted on to his shoulder. '*Daru-beedi!*' the parrot screeched. '*Eau de vie et tabac!*'

The men laughed again, and asked Lola something. She answered with a whistle that sent Suka fluttering towards her.

'They want to know if your talking parrot is tame,' she explained to Sam. 'I said he's so tame he'll go to anyone who whistles!'

Sam opened his mouth to protest. This was not true – Suka rarely went to anyone else. But if he told Lola this, she'd be even more pleased with herself.

'Shall we go, then?' he asked, slinging a bulky pack over his shoulders and walking to the canoe. 'It'll be dark soon.'

The Collector nodded. 'Let's make the best of it. Lola, tell these fellows – what are their names? – to load the packs.'

'You can call them both John,' Lola said.

'Surely they don't have the same name?'

'No, but that's what you can call them. John 1 and 2, if you prefer.'

The men stacked a pack each on their heads and stepped into the rocking canoe, balancing easily. They helped Lola and Sam board but the Collector waved them off and landed with a jump so heavy that the canoe tipped. With a swish of the wooden paddles, they were off, Suka flying ahead like a green arrow as the boat skimmed over the river.

'Tricky!' the Collector harrumphed. 'Bit of advice – give these people hooch and baccy, and they'll do anything. Savages! They're all the same. I've travelled to every continent – I ought to know.'

Sam flinched. Lola was at the prow of the boat and could hear every word.

'Still, it's worth it. I shall be the first man to penetrate this far into the Isle's interior. Ought to make *The Times*,' the Collector went on.

Sam looked at the Johns, confused. Did the Collector not think they were men?

The canoe swept on. After an hour, the muddy river had narrowed to a creek and the water, brownish with silt, became strewn with branches and logs. The boat's progress was sluggish, as the Johns pushed aside debris with their paddles.

Sam started at a sudden movement on the riverbank. What he'd taken for a knobbly log opened its jaw to reveal a ragged row of ivories. A crocodile! And one with longer, more vicious teeth than the wide-muzzled muggers he was used to. He watched it lurk at the water's edge, distracted only by the Johns, who were arguing again.

Lola turned to explain. 'Their boat won't go any further. The storm's blown too many trees into the water. We'll have to tie the canoe up and walk the rest of the way.'

Seven

Sam felt happier on dry land – he was a land pirate, after all, and his nomadic tribe were once hunters, whose forest homeland had mostly been cut down. He looked around, noticing how different the Isle was from the forests he knew. Sticky yellow mud caked his sandals, not like the dusty red earth of Indica, and the undergrowth's ferns and grasses brushed his knees. Even the tree trunks were a vivid green, snaked with vines and creepers. He sniffed the salty breeze and listened to the sounds it carried: stirring leaves, cicadas rasping and the hooting of wood pigeons.

The two Johns, loads balanced effortlessly on their heads, led the way, their machete blades swishing. They reached a narrow muddy track between the trees. It was humid – Sam's thin shirt was soaked – and he felt a sharp sting on his leg. Even the leeches here were fatter than back home. He picked off one that had suckered on to his ankle and threw it from the path. The Collector jumped.

'What was *that*?'

'Nothing, sir. Only a leech.'

'You're a quiet one, Sam Singh,' Lola remarked.

'Why d'you say that?'

She lowered her voice. 'You spotted that saltie back at the river! But you didn't make a fuss. And you picked off that leech like it was nothing.'

'I'm no city boy,' Sam told her.

'I know.'

'How? Because I'm not bothered by leeches?'

'I can tell by your walk. Knees bent, feet apart, looking down to check for tree roots and snakes. Not striding along, staring at the sky like—'

The Collector tripped, sprawling over and landed face down in a puddle.

'—like *him*,' Lola finished.

The Collector roared. 'This infernal isle!' he spluttered. The two Johns laughed as they helped Sam heave him to his feet. His face and hair were coated with thick yellow mud. 'It spat at me, I tell you. That *puddle* spat at me!'

Sam took a towel and water canteen from his pack and began to clean off the worst of it. He stared down at where the ground heaped up and muddy liquid bubbled and splashed.

'That's a mud volcano,' Lola told him. 'You get lots here. The mud's meant to be good for your skin!' She smiled encouragingly at the Collector.

The man shrugged Sam off. 'That's enough, boy. Did you say a mud volcano? Fascinating! Do your tribe have a name for them? What's their explanation – for example, is the earth angry?'

Lola shrugged. 'Don't know. Ask my grandfather, the village chief. He knows everything.'

'Of course! The child was raised in town. She won't know,' the Collector muttered. He wandered away, settling on the root of a banyan tree, taking a tin of tobacco – the good tobacco, Sam noticed – to fill his pipe.

'I have my own name for them, actually. I call them farty puddles!' Lola announced as the mud volcano emitted a wet, popping noise.

The Collector didn't hear her, but Sam did. He tried not to laugh, but the harder he tried, the more his laughter bubbled within him, until he was shaking with its force.

'It wasn't *that* funny,' Lola said, but by now she was laughing too.

Farty puddles! Tears welled in Sam's eyes and his middle ached – a good ache, not the griping belly pain of seasickness. How long had it been since he'd laughed – really laughed? Not since he'd left home. Or was it before Moon had disappeared? The two of them had laughed together all the time.

The two Johns joined in the fun. John 1 stood straight, marching a few steps and mimed tripping like the Collector. He slapped his thigh to mimic the sound of a face planted in mud, and they laughed even harder.

Clouds of tobacco smoke drifted over from the Collector.

'Don't mind him. The smoke will keep the bugs off while we sit here,' Lola said. 'We add a bit of tobacco to our fires, especially after the rains.'

'Is that why the Johns wanted it?'

She nodded. 'And alcohol's good for cleaning cuts and grazes. John 1's son hurt himself on a machete out hunting.'

The path widened until it was broad enough for Sam and Lola to walk comfortably side by side. Warm light reached between the rustling trees to touch their faces, tinting them crimson. Sam wondered how far they were from the village. Soon it would be dark, and darkness in a strange land was different from back home. He tensed at a sudden rustling and a musky animal scent.

'Only a civet cat,' Lola said, as if she knew what he was thinking. 'Probably has its home in that big peepal tree. They're harmless. Can I ask you something, Sam Singh? What's that mark on your arm? I noticed it on the canoe.'

Sam looked down at the tattoo inked on his inner forearm.

We are kings of the forest.
Let them tame us if they can!

'This? Oh, a scorpion. My—' He hesitated. *My brother has one too*, he wanted to say, but instead told her, 'My people are tattooed as babies. Boys with a scorpion, girls a fish. With thorns and an ink, made from special leaves. It's meant to protect us.'

Lola nodded. 'We have tribal marks to protect us too. But they don't stay for ever, they're made fresh each morning with clay.' She frowned. 'Your tattoo reminds me of something. I'll show you when we get to the village.'

As they talked, Sam found himself opening up, as if their laughter had cracked the hard carapace he'd grown since Moon left. He told Lola of his tribe: how they were hunters, woodcarvers, tattooists – and sometimes thieves, depending on need. His mother was the best tattooist in the tribe and Moon the best thief, though he didn't say this to Lola. He didn't feel ready to tell her about his missing brother yet.

Sam talked of hunting in his homeland, sparse now that logging had destroyed the forest. He'd spend days and nights tracking a single deer or wild pig under the full moon. Last month he'd almost speared a pig when a snake crossed his path, which meant bad luck. He'd returned empty-handed.

When Sam's father died, the brothers hunted together at first. But as Moon grew older, he'd found more profitable ways to spend his time. As they travelled, tents on their backs, cooking pot and tinderbox strapped to the donkey, Moon would vanish at night and return with his pickings: money, jewellery, or more likely a scrawny chicken and a clutch of eggs.

After Moon disappeared, Sam began hunting alone, helping to feed them whenever his stepfather had drunk away his wages. It was a long time since he'd had company in the forest, except for Suka.

As the sun sank low, the air came alive with a cacophony of squawks and thrum of wingbeats. Sam looked up to see a vast flock of green birds with long tails and tapered wings sweeping over the canopy.

'The parrots!' Lola exclaimed. 'They come to this part of the forest every night to roost. Bet your Suka's with them.'

A moment later, they heard the cry. '*Samudra Singh! Sam for short!*' as Suka alighted on Sam's shoulder, pecking his ear.

'*Ow!*' Sam laughed with relief. 'You found me, Suka! Have you made friends with the others?'

'*Friend! Ami! Dost! Nanban!*' agreed the parrot.

'*Milale,*' Lola added. 'That's our word for friend, Suka.' She grinned at Sam. 'We're close now. There's our cooking fire in the distance.'

Sam sniffed the faint scent of woodsmoke. But when he peered through the twilight, he saw only a scattering of lights that dimmed and glowed.

'I can see fireflies?'

'No – further up, high on the hill!'

A smoky haze smudged the skyline; the comforting flicker of amber flames below it promised warmth and food. They had almost reached Lola's village and Sam was eager to see the place she called home.

Eight

They trudged up the steep, rocky track behind the others, stumbling with tiredness. As well as the civet cat, they'd seen green geckos scuttle away and ochre snakes, slinking through the undergrowth. Now it was Lola's turn to tell stories. Night fell quickly here, with only the glow of fireflies and a quarter moon to light the way. Sam knew the Isle was less dangerous than the forests of his homeland, where wolves and tigers roamed, but he liked hearing her clear voice ring out in the darkness.

Lola told him how her people believed fireflies guided the spirits of the dead. The dead did not leave the world altogether, but lived above it, in a realm of light and air. Only a few of the tribe – Lola was one of them – had the gift of seeing spirits.

'Everything solid – you, me, animals, trees and the village – is invisible to them, just as ghosts are to people. All spirits see is *light*. They're attracted to it, like moths. That's why the port is full of ghosts,' she said. 'Those electric lamps in the governor's house – spirits love them!'

'But where do they come from?' Sam asked.

Lola snorted. 'Half the prisoners locked up in the Octopus don't make it out alive. That's a lot of ghosts. Terrible things happen there, Sam Singh. There's a reason this is known as the Isle of Lost Voices.'

Sam turned back to stare at her in the gloom, his throat tightening. Terrible things happened in prison – but he didn't want to believe they happened to Moon.

'How do you know?'

'When our people are out fishing, they sometimes find messages from the prisoners.'

He gulped. 'What... kind of messages?'

'In glass bottles,' Lola hissed. 'Prisoners throw them over the sea wall, hoping they'll float towards their families on the mainland. But most of them wash up here. That's what I wanted to— Look, we're here!'

She broke into a run and Sam followed her up the slope, wondering. His heart ached at the thought of Moon flinging a desperate message over the high prison wall, only for it to be snatched away by the waves.

They had reached a clearing, on the flat summit of a hill. Eight huts with thatched roofs sat around a central space where a great cooking fire blazed. A suckling pig roasted on a spit; the two boys turning it yelled greetings as Lola sprinted past. Their faces were painted with yellow clay and woven grass skirts hung around their waists. Lola waved, shouting, 'Who killed the pig?' but kept running towards a hut set back in the clearing, below a grove of tall, spreading padauk trees. Sam saw a grey-haired man stoop to greet her. He had to be Lola's grandfather.

Suka swooped from his shoulder and circled the clearing. '*Milale!*' he squawked. '*Friend!*'

Sam heard angry voices and sighed. What were they arguing about now?

The Collector was addressing the Johns loudly. 'For the tenth time! Which. One. Is. My. Hut? And where can the boy fetch water? I want to wash and shave.'

The Johns put their heads together, talking in low voices. It seemed to Sam that they disagreed about who would host the Collector. *You take him*, John 1 was saying, pointing to a hut. John 2 shook his head and waved his hands. *Not me!*

Lola reappeared with a fresh garland of red flowers around her neck, followed by the grey-haired man. He wore a fringed headdress of palm leaves that gave him the air of a lion. Ochre lines spanned his face, radiating like the rays of the sun. Red string circled his waist and upper arms and a necklace of white bones hung around his neck.

The two Johns stopped. Each man placed his hands on Lola's grandfather's shoulders in turn. They bumped foreheads and murmured greetings. Sam saw the Collector scribbling in his notebook by the dim light of the fire. He waited for the man to pay his respects to Lola's grandfather, but he didn't even stand up.

Lola nodded to Sam. 'Copy the Johns,' she whispered. 'Grandfather's the village chief. You must greet him. Call him Tuke.'

Sam stepped forward, placing his hands on the old man's strong shoulders and inclined his forehead, to feel the answering tap of the chief's. Lola's grandfather smelled like leaves and earth, fire and smoke. To Sam, he smelled like the forest.

'Tuke, sir,' Sam said, not knowing if the old man understood his words. 'Thank you for allowing us to visit your village.'

Lola's grandfather murmured in return.

'*Milale!*' Suka squawked nervously from a nearby tree. '*Friend!*'

The chief laughed and pointed up into its branches, astonished at the parrot speaking his own language.

'Hello!' he proclaimed. 'Hello, milale!'

The two Johns huddled together, whispering. They beckoned to Lola who announced to the Collector: 'You can stay in Tuke's hut. It's the largest in the village. We have water for you to wash. I'll show you.'

The Collector looked pleased at this, though not as pleased as the two Johns. He jerked his head at Sam, who gathered the packs and followed Lola.

The floor inside her grandfather's hut was compacted earth with bamboo matting laid on top. The walls were woven strips of wood and there was no light, not even a candle. From the firelight, Sam made out a piece of driftwood attached to the rafters, like a shelf. It held an assortment of objects: weathered glass bottles, a large conch shell, and a human skull, decorated with the same red flowers that garlanded Lola's neck.

Sam heated water over the cooking fire in a small billy can and shaved the Collector with an ivory-handled razor. When he finished, the Collector waved him closer.

'This is a bit of luck,' he whispered. 'Did you see what was inside the old man's hut?'

Sam shook his head and handed him a towel.

'The skull of an ancestor! This is a tribe of *head hunters*! They only hold on to the most revered of their forebears. They believe it protects them. I think this old fella must be the tribe's shaman. Explains why he has the biggest hut.'

Sam wondered. Surely the Collector, of all people, had no right to call anyone a head hunter? To give the skull of an ancestor fresh flowers and pay it respect was one thing, but to take skulls belonging to other people was another. Every tribe had customs, which might seem strange to outsiders. In his own tribe, the tradition was for a father to give the dried pelt of his first kill to his eldest son, to keep him safe when hunting. Sam's mother hadn't kept that one going. Perhaps that accounted for Moon's bad luck.

The whole tribe gathered around the fire. Dinner was roasted wild pig, baked yams and jackfruit, washed down with tea brewed from smoky leaves and sweetened with honey. Sam couldn't remember eating anything better. In his own tribe, only the elders remembered days when they'd live off what was gathered and hunted. The children were wary at first, but soon lost their shyness and ran from their mothers to pull Sam's hair and point at Suka, who pecked happily at a yam skin.

After dinner, the Collector lit his pipe and scribbled his notes by the light of the fire. The Johns acted out his fall into the mud volcano, to loud laughter from the gathered villagers. As the fire died down, Sam went to the hut to unroll the man's bedding and secure his mosquito net. The Collector's stuff took up most of the space. He wasn't sure how they would all fit around it.

'You're to remain on guard overnight, boy. Time enough for you to catch up on sleep in the day. Got my pistol under my pillow. If anyone tries to rob me, I'll be ready.'

Sam marvelled at how little the Collector understood the world. No one would invite a guest into their home and then rob them! Even his own tribe of land pirates would never stoop to such betrayal.

Lola and her grandfather had strung their hammocks between the trees in the clearing, like many of the villagers. Suka perched on the roof of the hut and Sam settled across the doorway, pinching himself hard to stay awake. But it had been a long day, and eventually he slumped into a fitful sleep.

Nine

'Morning!'

Sam jumped at Lola's voice ringing in his ear.

'You're drooling, Sam Singh. Did you sleep well?'

Sam shook his head grumpily and wiped his mouth on his sleeve. 'Not much.' He shuffled out of the doorway and stretched his neck, which had a painful crick. 'I wasn't supposed to fall asleep,' he mumbled. 'The Collector told me to stay on guard.'

'Guarding what?' Lola scrunched her face, confused. 'Anyway, do you want to see how they do our face markings? It's my turn to be painted.'

Sam didn't need to check that the Collector was still asleep. Each of his rumbling, drawn-out snores was so loud their vibrations shook the hut. He looked around the clearing and whistled. 'I'll come. Have you seen Suka?'

Lola shook her head. 'He's most likely pecking at fruit and making parrot friends. He'll find us. Come on.'

Sam followed Lola into another hut, where a smiling lady greeted them. Lola lay on her back, and the woman dipped a stick in a pot of yellow clay, and began decorating Lola's face with a delicate pattern of waves.

'Show Noma *your* tribe's mark, Sam,' Lola told him. Sam rolled up his left sleeve obediently. Noma frowned and said something to Lola, who tried to answer but was told to keep still.

'I forgot to tell you!' she exclaimed, once the face painting was finished and the clay had dried. 'Where I saw your scorpion. On one of the glass bottles Tuke keeps in his hut.'

'A glass bottle – with a scorpion?' Sam asked. Stupidly, he pictured a coloured label, like on his stepfather's beer bottles.

'Yes – bottles with a message inside. Tuke keeps the ones the villagers find. I'm not allowed to touch them, in case…'

Sam understood, suddenly, what Lola meant. Could she really have seen a message from one of his tribe? Surely it was too much to hope it might be from Moon.

'Where?' He jumped to his feet.

'I'll show you.'

They ran back across the clearing, but when they got to Tuke's hut, the Collector was awake, and peeved that Sam had left. Sam was scolded and told to rig up a shelter and lug a tin bucket back with water from a nearby stream, so the man could wash. Then, he had to wave a peacock-feather fan to keep mosquitos away, while Lola taught the Collector words for *man*, *woman*, *child*, *fire*, *hunt*, *tree* and *pig*.

'I have to go now,' she said, after he had written them down. 'Grub gathering – for lunch.'

'Grubs for lunch?' The Collector looked disgusted. 'Luckily I brought my own tucker – tinned meat and biscuits.'

'Well, I hope you're going to share,' Lola told him. 'In the village, everyone helps hunt or gather food. We all eat together.'

The Collector snorted. 'You, boy – go with the girl and gather grubs. Do our bit for the tribe, but I want you here afterwards.'

'I'll show you the bottle later,' Lola whispered, as they peeled back the papery bark of a palm tree.

They ate the grubs for lunch, wrapped in leaves and roasted over the glowing embers of the fire. Sam had not tried grubs before, but when times were hard, his tribe ate whatever they could hunt or trap, including rats, snakes and jackals, so he wasn't fussy. They tasted good, crunchy and a little cheesy.

The Collector did not join them. When Sam returned to Tuke's hut, he found the man stretched out on his sleeping mat snoring, an empty tin of corned beef and a scattering of crumbs beside him. He had not shared his food with the others.

Silently, Sam padded over to the shelf. There were four glass bottles, two green and two clear. He reached up and turned them by their cork stoppers, careful not to disturb the sandy dust. Inside were scraps of fragile paper, messages of hope and despair, destined never to be read by those they were meant for. He lifted a bottle and held it to the light, trying to make out the pattern on the glass. There it was! A scorpion, scratched out in the style of his own tribal tattoo. That looked like Moon's work. His brother was skilled at etching broken glass, usually images of fish or birds. He'd file the edges smooth and his mother would thread them as pendants to sell.

Sam wiped off the dust and made out a few words scrawled in uneven letters on the yellowed scroll inside. He felt as if the floor had vanished and he was falling. Now he was almost certain Moon *had* been transported to the Isle of Lost Voices, ending up in the Octopus, the only place his brother feared.

The Collector snored loudly, startling Sam, the bottle almost slipping from his fingers. He placed it carefully on the shelf, then crouched beside the man, pretending he'd come to wake him.

'Sir, it's time.'

The Collector rubbed his eyes and pulled out his pocket watch. 'Two in the afternoon – why didn't you tell me, boy? We have work to do! It's pitch-black by six and they won't allow so much as a candle in their huts.'

He pulled the mosquito net aside. 'Fetch the girl. Same routine.'

Sam fanned the Collector as the man scribbled down more of the words Lola taught him – *life, death, night, day, rain, sea, house, machete, bow and arrow, blowpipe* and *spear*. It took all afternoon, Lola repeating each word several times before the Collector wrote it down. Then he asked lots of questions, muttering to himself.

'How do your people have so many words for

sea? Never mind, let's go on. Does *gange* only mean spear?'

Lola thought about this. 'It means a long piece of wood. Like a stick?'

'But what's the difference between a stick and a spear?'

Lola bumped her fist on her forehead. 'Well, a spear has a sharp end. In the old days it was polished stone, now we find metal on the beach and melt it to make spear tips—'

'*I* know the difference, but how do your people know if someone is saying stick or spear?'

Lola rolled her eyes. 'We just do! At hunting time, you fetch a gange. Spear. But if a snake gets in the hut, Tuke brings a gange – a big stick – to kill it.'

Sam closed his eyes while they wrangled. One part of him was here, listening, while the other was still in the half-dark of the hut, tracing the outline of the scorpion: pincered claws, segmented body and curled tail with poisoned tip.

He had only made out a few words, and couldn't be certain it was his brother's handwriting – Moon didn't write much – but what he'd read through the glass sounded a lot like him:

Dear Ma, Your no-good son—

Sam hadn't managed to see the rest.

The peacock-feather fan slipped from his hands to the floor. He crouched to retrieve it, knowing what he had to do. He would open the bottle and read the note without the Collector – or Lola's grandfather – finding out. And he'd do it tonight.

Ten

After a meal of green mangoes and the last of the pig made into curry, Sam waited eagerly for the Collector to fall asleep. His plan was to take the bottle from Tuke's hut and read Moon's message by the fire's glowing embers. It never completely went out; a resinous wood the villagers used kept it going all night.

At first the plan went well. Once he heard loud snoring, Sam tiptoed inside and slipped the bottle under his shirt. But back at the fire, he found the stopper stuck fast. He tried twisting it with his teeth but it wouldn't budge.

'What are you doing out here, Sam Singh?'

'*Aargh!* Don't sneak up on me like that, Lola!'

Lola's eyes widened as she saw what he held in his hands.

'The glass bottle – you found it! Doesn't it look like your tattoo?'

Sam took a deep breath. 'It *is* my tattoo. Lola – I need to tell you something. Will you promise to keep it secret?'

He had found his way to the Isle alone but now he needed help. In the three years since his brother had disappeared, this was the first time he trusted anyone enough to ask for it.

'Of *course* I won't tell anyone. Wait here…' Lola ran off, returning a moment later clutching leftover grubs. 'Snacks!' she said, holding them out. 'Now, tell me everything.'

Sam told her about Moon. How he'd looked after Sam when their father died, encouraging him to stay in school and make a better future for himself. How Moon had risked imprisonment to feed the family. And how his brother was one of the best land pirates in the tribe: quick, silent, skilled at scaling bare walls or slipping through locked doors. Any time the police got him, Moon slid out of his handcuffs and escaped before they'd taken him to the lock-up.

'Except that last time,' Sam told her. 'I knew he was planning something big, but he never told me what. Said it was safer that way. Next morning, I woke up and he wasn't back. Ma even went to the police, but they wouldn't help her.'

'You think he's in the Octopus?' Lola looked horrified.

Sam shrugged miserably. 'I think so.' He traced the outline of the scorpion on the glass bottle. 'I need to find out for sure, Lola. I have to read this letter. But the stopper is stuck fast.'

'Well, you'll have to get it out. And quickly!' she told him.

'*Hello, Sam!*' They both jumped. Silhouetted against the dying fire stood Tuke, the parrot perched on his shoulder.

'*Hello, Sam,*' Suka repeated.

Sam leaped to his feet, surprised. '*Suka!* Why are you bothering Tuke?'

The old man beamed and spoke to Lola.

'He called the parrot to him. They've been teaching each other words,' Lola explained. 'Tuke might be able to help – with your brother?'

Tuke settled cross-legged by the fire, Suka perched on his head to crown the palm leaf headdress. He pointed to the glass bottle in Sam's hands. Even in the firelight, Sam saw that Tuke did not look pleased.

'Tell him I'm sorry?' he whispered to Lola, hoping he hadn't got her into trouble. 'I should have asked before I touched it. But I have to know what happened to Moon and this message might tell me!'

Lola nodded. 'I'll explain.' She spoke with the old man, then turned to Sam.

'Tuke says you'd better open it up and see.'

'Really? Thank you so much—'

The old man motioned to move back and raised the bottle over his head. Suka flew to perch on Sam's shoulder. The glass bottle glinted amber in the light from the fire, then Tuke smashed it on to one of the flat stones that edged the firepit. The bottle broke to fragments and Tuke extracted the yellowed paper, handing it to Sam. He unrolled it with shaking hands, spreading it open to read by the flickering firelight:

Dear Ma,

Your no-good son here. Got caught, like you said. Worse, got transported. You won't know what that means, but it's worse than you can imagine. Don't know how many days' journey I am from you and S. This place is beyond any hell I heard of. But I'm getting out. No jail can hold one of ours, no mind what the guards tell us. They say you'd be better off cutting your own throat than trying to escape. They tell you the Isle is surrounded by pirate-infested waters. And if you do escape, the forest folk

*shoot you with their bows and arrows. Not
me, they don't!*
    *We are kings of the forest, let them tame us
if they can!*

Sam felt something shatter inside, all at once,
like the glass bottle with its message. He realised
that, until now, a part of him had hoped his fears
were unfounded, that Moon had simply taken off,
roaming free.

    We are kings of the forest.
    Let them tame us if they can!

Moon hadn't written his name on the letter. But
that was the greeting their tribe called to fellow
travellers in his homeland.

    'It is him,' he told Lola, blinking away tears and
hoping she wouldn't notice in the darkness. 'It's
from my brother. He wrote it inside the Octopus.'

    *What's the worst that can happen, eh, Sam?
Transportation!*

    Lola's eyes widened. 'Tuke wants to know what
you found. Can I tell him?'

    Sam nodded. He read the letter to himself
again, while Lola explained to her grandfather.
A wisp of hope, thin as the smoke from the

firepit, curled inside him. From the letter, Moon had been planning to escape. Maybe he'd succeeded! But then why hadn't he come home or sent word?

'Tuke will enter the spirit world to search for your brother!' Lola told him excitedly. 'He can talk with the spirits. He's our wise man. The governor calls it another word – shaman or something? But only if you give him permission.'

Sam didn't completely understand, but he nodded. 'I would be grateful for any help finding my brother, sir,' he told Tuke.

Lola spoke to her grandfather who nodded and got to his feet. Sam watched him stride off.

'We'll do it tomorrow. There's lots to prepare for when Tuke makes one of his journeys.' She crouched to pick up the pieces of shattered glass.

Sam bent to help her but she waved him away. 'I'll finish clearing up here. You go and rest.'

'Lola – you said before you weren't allowed to touch the glass bottles *in case.* In case what?'

She glanced up at him. 'Not the bottles, exactly – it's the letters. Words have power. Tuke's worried they might hurt me. He says I haven't learned to spend time in their world safely.'

'Who might hurt you?' Sam was more confused than ever.

Lola frowned. 'The *spirits*. Like I said, some don't make it out of the Octopus alive. Their ghosts can be vicious. That's why Tuke keeps the messages, so if a prisoner's spirit troubles our village, he can trace their words and set them free.'

Sam gulped. 'Does that mean Tuke thinks he's dead – my brother?'

'Think of it this way – he'll be able to tell you for certain that he's alive.'

Sam couldn't sleep that night. He lay across the threshold of Tuke's hut, worrying. Tomorrow, Tuke would travel into the world of dead spirits, and – if he had understood – search for Moon's among them.

Eleven

Next morning, the tribe's best hunters set off with Lola, both the Johns, and the boys who'd been turning the spit when they arrived. The women of the tribe walked deep into the forest to collect leaves and berries for the feast. Tuke had woken before dawn to go to a sacred place and clear his mind.

Sam wandered about aimlessly, anxious about what Tuke would discover. He'd been left behind with the Collector, who was cross because Lola was off hunting, until Sam explained what all the activity was for.

'You mean I'm to witness a shamanic ceremony?' The Collector cheered up immediately. 'That's excellent! I'll take notes and write the whole thing up for publication.'

The Collector's mood improved further when he realised Suka had already picked up several words of Lola's language, mainly related to food. Sam encouraged the parrot by feeding him jackfruit seeds as a reward but eventually Suka tired of this and soared off into the forest.

'A good morning's work,' the Collector mused. 'Unique example of the Psittacidae, that bird. And here comes the hunting party.'

'They've caught a big one!' Sam watched the hunters heave a fierce-looking wild pig into the clearing, its legs trussed to a bamboo stick. 'I'll go and help.'

He ran over and offered to scrape off the bristles, while Lola told him tales of the hunt, complete with dramatic gestures.

'Then, John 2 speared it right in the belly! He had to dive on the ground – almost got trampled to death!'

'It's a beauty, all right,' Sam said approvingly. He offered to gut the pig with the knife he kept strapped to his belt. Lola admired its ebony handle and keen blade.

'My brother gave it to me.' He felt a lurch of fear as he remembered what all this – the hunting and feasting – was for. Tonight, Tuke would go in search of Moon's spirit among the dead.

'*Yum!* More food!' Lola remarked, pointing to the mothers returning with the littlest children and carrying baskets of yams, jackfruit and grubs on their heads. 'Tuke needs to eat a lot to make him sleep for his journey,' she explained. 'But we all get to share the feast.'

'You mean the old chap's *asleep* during this shaman business?' The Collector had walked over to watch.

'Of course!' Lola looked surprised. 'How else would he travel to meet the dead, except in dreams?'

'I see!' The Collector took his notebook out and scribbled in it. 'I'll need you to explain to me what's happening.'

She shook her head. 'I'm not allowed to talk during the ceremony. I have to play the drum for Tuke.'

'A drum!' The Collector wrote eagerly. 'Does it help your grandfather enter the shamanic trance?'

Lola shook her head. 'No – but it's important. See, when he enters the spirit world, Tuke can't see us, or the village. But he can still hear the drumbeat. It's like the string of a kite tying him down, to stop him flying away for ever.'

Tuke returned from the forest at twilight, his face and body freshly painted with ochre clay. They ate earlier than usual; the old man putting away a huge amount of roasted pig, yams and jackfruit. There had been no midday meal, and Sam ate his fill, along with everyone else.

After the elaborate arrangements, the start of Tuke's journey was disappointing. The old man simply lay at the edge of the clearing on a bamboo mat scattered with red flowers. Moon's letter was pinned to his headdress and Lola sat beside him, playing a steady beat on her hand drum.

Tuke fell asleep quickly and began to snore, though not as loudly as the Collector had snored the night before. The man sat with Sam, pen poised. The rest of the tribe went about their business, burying the bones from the hunt and storing the leftover meat.

Sam waited. Above the clearing, the sky deepened to indigo and a chittering of birds rose from the trees. Darkness slowly settled on the forest, as clusters of golden fireflies darted and bloomed between the great trunks of the padauk trees.

And then it began. Lola closed her eyes and beat her drum faster. Suka returned from the forest, shooting into the clearing to land on Tuke's chest. Sam tried to wave him off, worried the parrot's sharp claws would wake him, but Lola frowned and shook her head.

'Leave Suka where he is! He's helping.'

Sam looked at Tuke with concern. The old man was no longer snoring evenly. His breathing came fast and ragged, as if he was being chased. Around the clearing, the trilling crickets and twittering birds died away to an eerie silence. For a moment, all was still, then a violent wind gusted through the village, stirring up the dying fire so it blazed forcefully. Tuke's palm leaf headdress flapped in the wind and straw blew from the thatched roofs. Lola's drum was beating so fast it whirred in her hand. The villagers were silent. Tuke's body began to shudder frantically, like someone in the grip of fever.

Suka squawked a loud cry, and Lola called out, '*Tuke!* Come back to us.'

'What's the matter? Is he all right?' Sam gasped in alarm.

The old man's eyes opened. He lifted his head and stared about him, wide-eyed, then slumped back on to the mat. Lola's drumbeat slowed and ceased.

Two women ran over with a blanket of woven grass and Sam helped them lay it across Tuke. One squeezed the juice of small yellow berries into his mouth, which revived him enough to sit up. He yawned, shook his head groggily, then spoke to Lola in a hushed whisper.

'What happened? What did he see?' the Collector demanded.

Lola frowned. 'I'll explain tomorrow. My grandfather is tired, and his spirit is weak. I need to guide him to his hammock. Sam, come and help.'

Holding his arms, they walked Tuke past the smouldering fire. Sam glanced at Lola. He had to ask, though he wasn't sure he wanted to know what Tuke had discovered. The villagers gathered, waving them both away and took the old man into one of the huts.

'They're relieved to see my grandfather on his feet,' Lola told Sam. 'He's older now, so spirit journeys are riskier for him.' She handed him Moon's letter.

'You felt that powerful wind? That was the spirits, coming right through our village. No wonder everyone was worried.'

Sam swallowed. 'Did – did he see Moon?'

Lola shook her head. 'Your brother's not in the spirit world. That means he's *alive*. Good news!' She yawned. 'He'll tell us more tomorrow.'

Sam nodded and walked back to the hut alone. He could hear the Collector moving about inside, so he waited until all was quiet, then settled himself in the entrance.

Moon was alive. That *was* good news. But he was locked away in the Octopus. Which was bad. Unless Moon *had* escaped... but if he had, where was he now? Sam patted his pocket which held Moon's letter and shivered, remembering its warning words: *They say you'd be better off cutting your own throat than trying to escape.*

He stared up from the clearing, beyond the shadowy trees to the circle of night, where stars blazed a silver-white trail. He'd never seen the Akasaganga, the river of heaven, as clearly as here on the Isle, away from man-made light.

'Brother,' he whispered. 'Where are you?'

'You know where he is, dummy!' Lola's voice hissed. 'He's in the Octopus.'

'Lola! You made me jump!'

There was a muffled giggle and Lola appeared from the trees.

'I had to bury the flowers from the ceremony so the spirits don't return to the village. Aren't you pleased your brother's alive?'

Sam nodded. He looked back into the hut to check all was silent. 'Lola,' he whispered, 'Moon said in his letter he was planning to escape. I know the guards tell the prisoners it's impossible to break out because…' He trailed off. *If you do escape, the forest folk shoot you with their bows and arrows.* Surely that wasn't true?

Lola settled cross-legged beside him. 'It *is* impossible. Prisoners don't know how to survive in the forest. Some of our people have found them wandering, lost, and taken them back to prison. The authorities pay us well for escaped convicts. Stuff we need – matches, medicine, tobacco…'

'But, Lola…' Sam hesitated. 'Moon's not like those other prisoners. He's a genius at escaping. And he knows how to survive – how to hunt, how to move at night. Suppose he did get through this forest – where would he go next?'

'There isn't anywhere for him to go! He couldn't board a ship from the port or they'd arrest him. And the north of the Isle belongs to the Jalai Rajah, king of sea pirates. Even the governor's men won't sail his shores. I feel sorry for any convict who makes it that far.' Lola clicked her teeth and mimed slashing her throat. 'I know Moon's your brother, but he's better off inside the Octopus.'

Sam sighed. He'd been so afraid Moon was a prisoner, but now it seemed that was the best fate he could hope for. 'I need to find him, Lola. I know outsiders think our tribe's ways are wrong. But we only steal from those who won't miss a chicken or a few coins—'

Lola shrugged. 'I don't care about that! We don't live like townspeople. Imagine if I found a nest of bees and said no one could eat their honey but me, or they'd be stealing. Everyone would laugh themselves silly!' She scrunched her face. 'Are you *sure* your brother didn't do anything worse?'

Sam shook his head. 'Moon would never hurt anyone.' *Not unless something was badly wrong*, he added to himself.

Lola hesitated. 'Just now, as he was going to sleep, Tuke did say something else. Moon's spirit wasn't with the dead so he searched for him among the living. That's hard, but he did see a dim light before he had to return. Tuke's old, so the spirit world's pull is strong.'

Sam thought over what she'd said. 'A dim light? Does that mean he's sick?'

Lola shook her head. 'From what Tuke's taught me, a dim spirit means a person's sad or sick...' She glanced at Sam. 'Sick in his *mind.*'

Sam was unsettled by this new fear. He'd heard prisoners in the Octopus were handcuffed, shackled and beaten. *Terrible things happen there.* What if Moon had given up hope completely? If his brother *was* in the Octopus, Sam had to see him

– or at least pass him a message. Moon needed to know he hadn't been forgotten.

'I'll have to go back, Lola!' he whispered urgently. 'Back to the port to find the Princess of Moonlally. Remember, Sparrow said she's on the Isle to visit the jail? I bet if I ask, she'll pass on a letter. I must help Moon!'

Lola frowned. 'All right. I can guide you back to the port in the morning.' She nodded into the hut, taken over by the Collector. 'But what are we going to do about *him*?'

Twelve

Just then, the Collector stepped out of the hut. 'Glad to see you're both ready to set off! I thought we'd leave for the port, bright and early.'

'Now?' Lola gave Sam a confused look. 'Before daybreak? But don't you need to hear more from Tuke about his spirit journey? He won't wake until much later.'

'All the better.' The Collector peered into the empty clearing. 'Let's not bother the old man. We can be ready by first light. I'm keen to get back to civilisation and write this up for the Anthropological Society.'

Sam exchanged glances with Lola, hoping he hadn't overheard their conversation. Was it a coincidence that Sam needed to return to the port, and by some miracle, so did the Collector? He sprang to his feet. 'Yes, sir. But – shouldn't we tell the others we're leaving?'

The Collector lowered his voice. 'No need to disturb everyone, eh? You guide us to the river, Lola – from there, the boy and I can manage the canoe.'

'It's still dark! And we haven't had breakfast,' Lola objected. 'Plus, it's going to rain – the spirits Tuke summoned have brought on a storm.'

'Pfft! You're not scared by a little rain? Look, I'm leaving one of the packs behind. Plenty of bully beef and biscuits, a good bottle of Scotch and some decent tobacco in there. That ought to compensate the Johns for their canoe.'

Sam frowned. The Collector was behaving oddly. He looked unusually cheerful, even their protests hadn't wiped away the man's fixed smile.

'It's not the canoe... they can easily make another one.' Lola shrugged. 'All right, then.' She raised an eyebrow at Sam. 'Might be for the best if you go back to town?'

'Jolly good. Since that remarkable parrot has picked up the local lingo, I can work on my dictionary in comfort at the Residence.'

Sam felt uneasy. Sneaking away without saying goodbye seemed wrong. They ought to thank the villagers for their kindness, the food they'd shared and their hospitality in giving up Tuke's hut.

But Moon was the reason he was on the Isle. He needed to find Sparrow and the Princess of Moonlally, and quickly – they were only here until the *Yellow Pearl* sailed. He nodded at Lola. 'I'll pack your things, sir.'

'No need. I've taken care of it. Lola – are you ready? You'll be back before your grandfather wakes if we leave now.'

They began their trek to the whooping hoot of a lone owl. As they descended, the skies flooded red and the jungle birds began their raucous dawn chorus. Sam recognised the whistles of bulbuls and squawking cries of treepies. He looked up at Suka, who flew silently above their small party and wondered if the parrot was sad to leave the lush forest with its teeming birdlife – he knew he was. Glancing up the path towards the village, he saw smoke drifting from the fire.

'Look sharp now, no dawdling!' the Collector called as he strode along. Sam adjusted the straps of his pack and walked faster. Despite emptying most of the tins, it felt heavier than when they'd arrived.

They hiked down the jungle slopes towards the river. Soft trails of grey began to streak the pink sky.

'Told you it was going to rain,' Lola announced. 'Look at those clouds!'

87

'Call those miserable things clouds?' the Collector scoffed. 'Nonsense!'

They made their way through dense forest and down the narrowing track. Lola stopped. 'This path soon turns towards the sea. We'll need to look for the machete marks to find the way we came from the river. And the light's fading.'

Sam looked up. The sky was now a mottled silver, blanketed in thick cloud. Suka had flown ahead, and now returned, shrieking, '*Storm, toofan, tempête!*'

A flock of parrots spiralled into the grey and Suka joined them. Sam knew he didn't like the rain and would take shelter in the trees.

'Let me get to a lookout and see how far off the storm is. Wait here!' Lola called, climbing a nearby tree.

Sam watched, anxiously tracking her progress from the shaking branches and rustling leaves. It wasn't a good idea to be up a tree if lightning struck.

'It's going to be huge!' she yelled down. 'I can see black rain clouds moving in from the shore. We need to take shelter!'

'But that will slow us down!' the Collector complained, as she scrambled back on to the ground. 'Shouldn't we keep moving?'

'We're not too far from where we make camp in the dry season,' Lola told him. 'Let's head that way.'

As they hurried on, the sky grew darkly overcast and thunder rumbled. Rain fell in great silver drops, becoming scattered bursts which swelled to a downpour. Yellow mud squelched under their feet, while green geckos skittered and red frogs hopped across the slick path.

'Watch out for snakes,' Lola warned. 'They wriggle out of the mudflats and up the paths when it's wet.'

They were soaked by the time they arrived at the camp, built on a raised platform of flattened earth. Unlike the village huts, with their cosy bamboo walls and thatched roofs, the shelters had only canopies of woven leaves, held up by large bamboo poles at each corner. One or two had already blown away in the storm. The largest shelter had a hole dug in the centre for a firepit and a heap of cooking pots.

'Don't rate this!' the Collector snorted. 'We'd be better off under a tree!'

'Not if it's struck by lightning,' Lola muttered. 'This camp's only temporary,' she explained. 'We build it fresh every dry season. I'm surprised there's so much left.'

They dumped the packs and Lola found a pile of damp brushwood and lit a smoky fire. She unrolled a bamboo sleeping mat from a pile and yawned, gesturing at the rain dripping from the roof edges and running down the bamboo pillars.

'We're not going anywhere until this stops. Might as well get some sleep.'

The Collector grunted but took out his own bedroll and did the same.

Sam knew he wouldn't be able to sleep. His mind was too full of questions about his brother. He needed to move, so decided to explore, despite the rain falling in silver plumes.

Built at the edge of the forest, the dry season camp was close to a low cliff, with steps cut into the rock leading down to the beach. Sam made his way to the edge and sat on the top step. He could see the rolling breakers and hear the seabirds' cries. A tall grey heron took off from the water's edge with a long, haunting call. Rain poured down on him in sheets, but he didn't care.

He knew Moon was alive, and – he hoped – still in prison, his spirit dim. But wouldn't anyone feel that way, locked up in the Octopus? He was sure if he could only see his brother face to face, Moon would recover.

As he stared past the waves to the seething expanse of water and horizon beyond, something broke the surface. A great curved shape, its skin shining with a metallic gleam. He heard a dreadful whirring groan, followed by a clanking sound. Could it be a whale, or some other giant sea creature? He'd heard about whales but had never seen one. But this sound was like no animal – it was almost *mechanical*. Sam stared in wonder as a hole – or a window, like the glass portholes on the *Yellow Pearl*, slid open at the crest of its back. He heard a rushing of air, then it slid shut and the strange contraption sank once more beneath the surface.

Sam blinked and rubbed his rain-streaked eyes. Where had it gone? If it was a ship, it was the strangest he'd ever seen. Could it be a whaling vessel? It had the same silvery, curved shape as a sea creature – perhaps it was made to hunt them? Shaking his head, he scrambled to his feet and headed back to the shelter to ask Lola.

He returned to find Lola and the Collector both asleep. The small fire was smoking and almost out. He stoked it with more wood and sat close by, his clothes steaming as he dried off.

Lola woke not long after. Her eyes blinked open, startled, and she sat up suddenly, clapping her hand to her heart. 'Whew! Good job keeping the fire going, Sam Singh. I had such a strange dream!'

'What was it about?'

'My great-great-uncle Onay. He was our chief, and a shaman, just like Tuke. He was *furious*. Shouting, jumping up and down, pointing!'

'Does he not usually behave that way?'

Lola shook her head. 'Normally, he's very peaceful. He only appears in my dreams when I'm at the village, and he always gives good advice. At the port, they're plagued with angry spirits; I never sleep properly when I'm there. But Uncle Onay's not like that.' She shook her head. 'I don't know *what* he was so mad about!'

'What about that horseman – the colonel who gallops around the Residence – is he a good spirit or a bad one?'

Lola waggled her hand. 'Old Mayo? Somewhere in between. He's been around so long he doesn't cause trouble. Everyone at the Residence is used to him, they sleep through his noise.'

'Why does he gallop about like that?'

'Spirits stay close to where they lived or died. The Residence was once his home. See, if you die peacefully, surrounded by family, you end up as a good spirit. If you suffer a violent death, that makes your spirit *angry*.' She shivered. 'That's why our people don't go near the port if they can help it.'

'Did Uncle Onay die peacefully?'

'Yes – at home in the village, with his family. You've met him, sort of. Onay's skull is kept in Tuke's hut, filled with fresh flowers. He's one of our most respected ancestors.' She stood up and stretched. 'I only wish I knew why he was so cross! Anyway, what have you been doing, Sam Singh?'

'I went to the cliff edge and looked out to sea.' Sam frowned. 'Listen, Lola, do enormous sea creatures travel through these waters, like whales? Do you get whaling boats?'

Lola shook her head. 'Never seen a whale. We get dugongs in the mangrove swamps around the shore. But I haven't heard of whaling boats near the cliffs. That bay's shallow for a good way out. Why d'you ask?'

Sam described what he'd seen and Lola looked mystified.

'Are you sure it wasn't a pirate ship? I told you deadly sea pirates patrol this stretch of coast. We keep a canoe on that beach – these are good fishing waters, but the pirates leave us alone. We don't have stuff worth stealing.'

'A canoe, you say?' The Collector was awake. 'I have an idea! What if the boy and I paddle south around the Isle instead of trekking? We'll get to the port faster than slashing our way through the jungle to where we left the other boat?'

Lola frowned. 'That's not a good plan. The storm may have died down, but tides are strong. Unless you're experienced, it's easy to lose control and drift out to sea. And like I said, there are pirates.'

'Those miserable sea pirates wouldn't dare touch me. No harm taking a look, eh? Boy, you tidy up.'

Lola sighed. The Collector was as insistent as ever. 'All right! I'll take you to the cliff edge and you can see for yourself. At least it's stopped raining.'

Sam put out the fire, swept the floor of the shelter and tidied away the bamboo mats. He picked up the Collector's khaki bedroll. Why *was* he in such a hurry to get back to the port? He shook his head, struck by the odd way he'd made them leave so suddenly.

As he replaced the bedroll in the Collector's pack, he noticed, to his surprise, the bag was almost empty. There was his shaving kit, a fountain pen and his pipe with a tin of tobacco, and below that, a box of lightly varnished wood. Curious, Sam lifted it out. He didn't remember seeing it before among the Collector's things. He undid the brass latches and cautiously lifted the lid.

Inside lay Uncle Onay's skull, red petals clinging to the bony vault.

Thirteen

S am slammed the lid shut. Now he understood
Lola's distressing dream – no wonder Uncle
Onay was cross! He needed to tell her what the
Collector had done. Stealing the remains of an
ancestor was terribly wrong.

But if he did tell her, how would the man react?
He remembered the pistol, tucked into the front
pocket of the Collector's safari jacket. If Lola
demanded the return of Uncle Onay, might he
threaten her?

Voices carried over the crash of waves and he
hurriedly finished packing.

'It's too risky,' Lola was telling the Collector.
'Did you see the size of those waves? The currents
in the bay are strong and I don't know them like
the fishermen. Also – like I said – *pirates*!'

'Nonsense! The waves are only at the shore – out in the bay it's flat as a board. A heave-ho and we'll be rounding the coast and in sight of the port in no time. The Isle's barely 16 kilometres long!' He nodded at Sam. 'Come on, lad! Give me my pack.'

Sam passed the Collector the lighter pack and shouldered the heavier one himself. What could he do? He decided to drop back and tell Lola as they walked to the beach. If he asked the Collector to return Uncle Onay, he wouldn't listen. They'd have to confront him together.

He followed the others along the clifftop until they reached the steps leading to the beach. The sea was still, the tide half-out. The silver-grey volcanic sand was washed smooth, but scattered branches lay at the treeline and one or two slender palms had been toppled by the storm.

'The canoe's over here. We keep it above high tide mark, so we'll need to carry it to the water.' Lola led them into the trees, where a canoe, smaller than the dugout the two Johns used, was roped to a broad trunk. Narrow, with a curved hull, a flat bow and stern, it held a bamboo pole and two pairs of wooden paddles. The three of them lifted the boat and staggered back to lay it at the shoreline.

'Now, I'll get in and you both push the canoe slowly out,' the Collector commanded. 'Boy, wade alongside and jump in once we're properly afloat.'

They did as he said. It took a surprising effort to move the boat with the Collector inside.

'Come on, put your back into it!'

The water was at Sam's waist now. He took off the heavy pack and placed it in the bottom of the boat to keep dry.

'Use that pole to push yourself out!' Lola told him. 'There's one in the canoe. I'm going back to shore and Sam can't wade any further – or he'll be swimming!'

The Collector lifted the bamboo pole used for guiding the boat in shallow waters. 'Let's shove this driftwood here out the way – *aargh*!'

A gigantic mud-coloured head surfaced with a roar. The saltwater crocodile's jaws opened and it clamped ragged teeth over the canoe, tipping it sideways.

Lola screamed. She grabbed a paddle, stumbling backwards into the water. 'Your pistol, sir!' Sam yelled. 'Use your *pistol*!'

The Collector was clinging to the side of the tilting boat. He patted uselessly at the pocket of his safari jacket, his face frozen with fear.

GITA RALLEIGH

The canoe angled more steeply, and one of the packs slid into the sea. Sam knew he had to do *something*. Any moment now, the crocodile's seized-up jaws would ease open and they'd be targets.

Lola was on her feet again, holding her paddle high. 'Stay back, Sam!' she shouted. 'I'm going to whack it!'

'Hang on!' Sam grabbed the knife from his belt and leaped on to the saltie's armoured head, plunging the blade deep into its hooded yellow eye. A watery, pinkish liquid squirted out. The reptile made a desperate, anguished groan, thrashing its tail and throwing Sam off. Its great jaws slackened, releasing the canoe from their grasp. Sam scrambled on board as Lola struck the paddle down hard on the beast's muzzle and the crocodile bellowed. The waters heaved with the power of its flailing tail as it swam off, leaving the canoe juddering.

The Collector's face was pale. 'Whisky!' he called. 'Boy, get me the— Dash it, left it at the village. Which pack went in the water?'

'It was the heavy one, sir.' Sam could see the pack, drifting along in the shallows.

The Collector seized the remaining pack and lifted it. 'Good – this is the important one. Don't bother fetching it – let's cast off.'

He patted the outline of his pistol. 'Didn't need this in the end, did we? Never waste a bullet until you see the whites of their eyes.'

'You'd better not cast off in this,' Lola said grimly. 'The canoe isn't seaworthy now that saltie's taken a chunk out of it.'

Sam looked at the canoe edge, where the wood was splintered and broken.

The Collector scoffed. 'I'm rowing this boat around to the port.'

Lola pointed at the darkening sky. 'Look at those clouds! The wind's up and once the waves rise, you won't stay afloat – water's already seeping in.'

Sam could see the canoe drifting from the shore, the turquoise water below darkening. Grabbing the pole, he pushed it into the seabed, hoping the one-eyed croc wasn't lurking nearby.

'A bit of advice?' Lola called through gritted teeth. 'Don't blame *me* when you get taken by pirates! If you see the Jalai Rajah's red skull-and-crossbones, you're better off in the sea – crocs and all!' She vanished into the water, swimming swiftly towards the beach.

'Lola – wait!'

Sam drove the pole deeper into the seabed. He couldn't let Lola go without telling her about Uncle Onay – it wasn't right.

'Sir – what if that crocodile's on shore? I need to check Lola's safe.'

'The girl's fine. I can't wait any longer – the tide's taking us out!'

'Here's an anchor.' Sam lifted a lump of coral, bound with rope and attached to the hull. 'I'll go and check on her and then we'll set off. Keep your pistol ready, in case the saltie comes back!'

The Collector looked furious, but Sam knew he'd realise the canoe would be difficult to handle alone. 'Off you go, then. Quick now!'

Sam gripped his knife between his teeth and paddled to shore, stopping to grab the pack and drag it on to the sand. He wasn't as strong a swimmer as Lola. She was already further up the beach, making for the trees. He placed the pack carefully on a rock and sprinted to catch her.

Fourteen

'*L*ola!' he called. 'Lola, wait!'

She turned but kept running.

'I need to tell you something!'

'Tell me up here!' Lola called, as she began scaling a tree, limber as an acrobat, making for a wooden platform built across its branches. She slid over to sit on the edge, high above him, swinging her legs.

'Sam Singh!' she pointed accusingly. 'I saw what you did. Quiet as a mouse, with all that "yes, sir, no, sir" – and then – *whoosh!*' She raised her hand and brought it down in a stabbing motion. 'Knifed the beast right in its eye! You saved that fool of a Collector's life.'

'*Sam Singh!*' A parrot squawked above them, before wheeling away into the flock. They both craned their necks. Lola whistled and then called. '*Su-ka!*'

Sam shook his head wonderingly. 'I'm... not sure it was Suka? That wasn't his voice.'

''Course it was! We don't have talking parrots on this Isle.'

Sam didn't answer. He was concentrating on clambering up towards her, careful of his handholds. Lola was a better climber as well as a stronger swimmer. But Sam was a better hunter, only because he'd had to do it alone since Moon had gone. He could tell Lola was absorbing this new, crocodile-stabbing side of Sam into the picture she had of him.

'Look down there, Sam Singh,' she said, when he finally reached the platform. She waved towards the water. 'I told you that Collector was a fool. He's only gone off without you!'

Sam looked. The small canoe was already a fair way out to sea. Either the man had lifted the anchor, or the coral hadn't held against the waves. The clouded skies were darkening and thunder boomed low again. They watched the grey sea churn and foam as the Collector paddled in vain; the canoe was drifting further and further from shore.

Lola shrugged. 'I *told* him! You heard me, didn't you? I warned that the storm wasn't over.'

Huge pearly raindrops began to pound at the shelter's roof, woven from leaves. Water slid off and dripped down the edges.

'We should get back on the ground,' Sam said. 'What will happen to him?'

Lola sighed. 'If he doesn't drown, or meet the one-eyed croc, he'll be taken by the pirates. They won't kill him though – they'll demand a ransom. The governor's not going to be happy.' She yawned. 'I'm *so tired*, Sam Singh. I wish I knew why Uncle Onay was in such a rage. What did you want to tell me, anyway?'

Sam grimaced. 'I think I might know why. See, back at the Residence, I got to wondering what was in the Collector's big case. It was packed with skulls, Lola! *Human* skulls. Someone's ancestors – and I'll bet they weren't the Collector's people.'

'No – they're particular about those. They lock them in a wooden box underground with a stone slab to stop them escaping. The governor's wife died ages ago, and he offers flowers every week to keep her spirit happy. But what's that got to do with Uncle Onay?'

Sam swallowed. He told her how the Collector had pointed out the skull in Tuke's hut. 'But I never thought he'd do this! Back at the camp, I was stashing his bedding away and wondered why his pack was half-empty. I looked inside and saw Uncle Onay in a box. The Collector *stole* him!'

The rain abated. Shafts of gold sunlight shone through the canopy of leaves and lit Lola's face, her eyes wide in shock.

'I *thought* it was strange he wanted to leave without waking anyone. Sam Singh – if Uncle Onay's lost, bad things will happen to our village! No wonder he was furious.

'He isn't lost.' Sam pointed to the pack still visible at the water's edge. 'I swapped Uncle Onay into *my* pack – the heavier one. It tipped from the boat when the crocodile attacked and I fished it out. Look, it's down there!'

'With Uncle Onay inside!' Lola began scrambling down from the platform. 'Come on, let's go and get him.' She hesitated. 'But what about… you know, the one-eyed saltie.'

'The tide's going out. We should spot the croc if it comes back. I'll keep my knife handy.'

Lola agreed, so they slid down and made for the beach. After fetching the pack, they climbed the steps to the top of the cliff, carrying Uncle Onay between them. The fierce sun's heat made their wet clothes steam as they trudged towards the camp.

Sam took out Uncle Onay. He was wrapped in the Collector's bedroll, and looked a little soggy but otherwise unharmed by his ordeal. Lola placed the skull by the smouldering firepit.

'There you go,' she said. 'That should dry him out nicely.'

They looked at Uncle Onay and then at each other.

'What now?' Sam asked.

'Sam *Singh*!' Lola started to laugh. 'You've stabbed a crocodile in the eye, rescued Uncle Onay and got rid of that annoying Collector. Don't you think we deserve to sit here, just for a minute? It's barely lunchtime!'

Sam realised he was ravenous. 'Let's eat. I stashed some cans over there.'

Lola nodded eagerly. 'I always think much better after food.'

They feasted on tinned sardines, washed down with a large bottle of tonic water from the Collector's pack, which made them burp.

'You'll have to take Uncle Onay back to the village,' Sam said, once they'd stopped burping and giggling.

Lola shook her head. 'But how will you get to the port on your own? You need to find your brother!'

'What if we take Onay back first, then you can guide me to the port?'

'It'll be too late. We'd have to stay in the village overnight. And Tuke will be cross about Uncle Onay – who knows if he'll let me go? You'll miss your chance to speak to the princess!' She stood up and stretched. 'Let's set off for the port now – the way we came, along the river – and take Uncle Onay. I think he'll be happy if I hold him.'

'Are you sure?' Sam felt his face grow warm. He was grateful, though uncertain, why Lola was going out of her way to help him. He was just another stranger, disrupting the peace of her tribe.

'Sam *Singh*! If it wasn't for you, that saltie would have mauled us both! *And* you saved Uncle Onay. Of course I'm sure.' She sighed. 'Besides, I need to tell the governor the Collector's in trouble. He'll send out a search party.'

'*Sam Singh! Sam Singh! Sam Singh!!*' A chorus of parrot cries sounded above them. They jumped to their feet and ran out of the shelter as the flock wheeled and swooped away, their bright emerald mingling with the deeper greens of the jungle.

'That *wasn't* just Suka...' Lola marvelled. 'A pandemonium of parrots, all calling out your name. What's going on?'

'I think Suka's teaching the others to speak? It sounds unlikely but—'

'Suka *is* a very clever parrot,' Lola finished, smiling. 'He'll find us, won't he?'

Sam stared up into the canopy. One day, Suka might not return. What if he was happier in the wild, here among his own kind? Sam would miss him, but Suka was his friend, and free to choose for himself.

They tidied away the remains of their meal, shook out the bedroll and hung it to dry, wrapping Uncle Onay's skull carefully in palm leaves. Lola held him facing outwards on her front, which felt more respectful. Then they set out for the river once more, hurrying to make the port before nightfall.

Fifteen

The storm clouds had ebbed to reveal a low red sun, and the evening birdsong was in full chorus by the time they reached the river. They found the Johns' canoe tethered to a tree. Brushing off loose leaves and twigs, they dragged it to the water's edge. The storm's downpour had transformed the river, washing away the fallen trees and debris. The green water was now high and fast flowing.

'Are we strong enough to paddle this?' Sam asked doubtfully, as they pushed it into the water and clambered on.

'We're rowing with the current, as it flows to the port and meets the sea,' Lola reminded him. 'It'll be easier than on the way here.'

The boat rocked a little then swung around, carrying them swiftly along. They took up their paddles and found a rhythm. Sam remembered the croc he'd seen on the way there and patted his knife, just in case.

'At least this canoe won't overturn,' Lola told him. 'The Johns are the best boat builders. They pick the right trees to dig out so the boat stays stable in rough water. And they use a special mix of pine resin and charcoal to waterproof it.'

Once in the main channel they made rapid progress, the canoe flying through the forest, the only sounds chirping crickets and their paddles swishing against the water. Fireflies flashed bright gold against the trees lining the riverbank.

'Firefly time,' Lola exclaimed. 'Sunset is when we build up the evening fire at the village and tell stories. My favourite time of day.'

'Did you always live in the village, Lola?' Sam asked. Hadn't the Collector said she was raised in the port?

Lola sighed. 'I don't like to talk about it. But you're all right, Sam Singh, so I'll tell you. See, when I was in my mother's belly, my parents caught a sickness from strangers visiting the village. The governor was one of them, though he didn't know he'd brought it.' She shook her head. 'My father died before I was born and my mother giving birth to me – and *I* nearly died too – I didn't cry for three whole minutes! Tuke was scared the villagers would think I carried the sickness. He took me to the port and knocked on the door of the governor's mansion for help. The governor promised to raise me there.'

'Did Tuke live with you?'

'No, but he visited every week when I was small. And when I was older, I went to live with him in the village. Tuke taught me to hunt, fish and gather food. Now I only come to the port if the governor needs me to translate for him.'

Lola was tiring; Sam could feel her strokes falter. The warm light of sunset had waned from the twilit sky; soon darkness would fall. A shadow swooped to land on the canoe, startling them both.

'Suka! How did you find us?' Lola cried.

'*Sam Singh! Lola!*' Suka hopped on to her shoulder affectionately.

She turned to gaze into the distance. 'I hope we're there soon. We need to look out for the light at the end of the pier, so we can moor the canoe.'

'You rest for a bit – I'll row,' he told her. 'Suka can help. Fly ahead, boy – come back and tell us when you see a light!'

Suka soared off at once, his cry fading into the air.

'I was very small when I first saw ghosts at the port,' Lola began. 'At first, I was scared. When

Tuke explained what they were, I longed to see my mother and father. But spirits who were loved hardly ever appear.' She shivered.

'My father died when I was little too.' Sam told her about his stepfather and new baby sister.

'You're lucky to have family. I only have Tuke, and he's old. He wants me to take over as shaman, but I still have so much to learn.' She yawned, curling up in the boat's hull. 'I might just close my eyes.'

Sam rowed on, feeling his arms begin to shudder with tiredness. Just as he was wondering whether they should tie the boat up and rest overnight, Suka wheeled back, crying. '*Light! Bijli, Lumiere, Oli!*'

Sam shook Lola awake and squinted through the gloom at the faint yellow lamp burning. 'Lola – I see it!'

He ploughed them into the bank and used the paddle to turn the prow towards the platform. Once the canoe was securely fastened to the mooring chains, they both climbed up and collapsed on to the wooden pier. Suka dived to join them, perching on Sam's head.

'Shabash, Suka! We'd have missed that light without you!' Sam reached up to scratch the parrot's neck.

Lola struggled to her feet, clutching Uncle Onay. 'The road's through those bushes. Let's keep going – it's an hour's walk to the port.'

They both froze at the unmistakeable low grumbling of an engine.

'Who's that – all the way out here?' she wondered.

'Doesn't matter – it's a *car*! They might give us a lift!' Sam sprinted through the undergrowth towards the road, reaching it just as the twin beams of its headlights swept around the curve.

'Hey!' he yelled, running after it, waving his arms. 'Stop! *Wait!*'

The shiny black car, a smaller version of the governor's, rumbled to a halt. Lola, who'd had to walk because of Uncle Onay, caught up with him as a door opened.

'Well, I never! If it isn't Samudra Singh!' A young woman stepped out, dressed in a white shirt, trousers and braces, her hair in a loose plait. She looked oddly familiar. 'Come on, Sam – Lola and Suka too!' She waved them closer. 'In you get – the back seat's empty!' When they hesitated, she added, 'I'm not sure what's happened, but you look exhausted! We'll give you a ride to the port.'

Sam and Lola climbed in and the other woman passenger turned and smiled as they set off, the headlights illuminating the twisting road through the hills.

Sam sank wearily into the leather seats. They were comfortably padded and there was even a blanket. He was so tired. He pulled the blanket over him and felt his eyes closing. But Lola sat bolt upright beside him, clutching Uncle Onay's skull.

'Sam *Singh*! Wake up—' She elbowed him sharply in the ribs. 'Who are these people? How do they know our names? I don't like it…'

Sam jerked awake and stared sleepily out of the window. They were rounding the hill. Far below were the clustered yellow lights of the port. A huge floodlight blinked from the watchtower of the Octopus, its white beam fanning into the night. Somewhere in that jail was his brother, Moon.

'I'm sorry,' he said, leaning forward. 'But do we know you?'

The young woman driving laughed. 'How silly of us,' she said. 'I forgot you wouldn't recognise me without my yellow turban and mooch! I was dressed as a servant boy last time we met. It's me – *Sparrow*.'

Sixteen

That night, Sam had terrors that made him sweat and thrash about in the narrow bunk. He dreamed he was swimming – he didn't know where to – and flailing desperately in the water, while a huge crocodile slid closer, its gnarled ivories snapping.

'No!' he yelped, and woke to find Suka pecking at his big toe.

'*Breakfast, nashtha! Petit déjeuner! Kalai unavu!*' Suka screeched.

Sam shook himself awake. He remembered he was at the bungalow with Sparrow and the princess, up the hill from the Governor's Residence. When they'd arrived late last night, he'd only seen a low white building, its wide verandah hung with bamboo blinds. Sparrow, noticing how tired he and

Lola were, had led them to a small bedroom with a couple of bunks.

'We'll talk in the morning!' she'd said firmly when Lola began explaining about the Collector.

Sam reached to scratch Suka, who was perching on his right foot, and sniffed the delicious smell of breakfast.

'Hungry, are you, Suka? Me too!'

He heaved himself out. The top bunk was empty. Through a wooden door, he could hear splashing. Lola pushed the door open and yawned.

'Sam *Singh*! We have our own bathroom – this place is *fancy*. I've been awake for ages, while you moaned and yelled in your sleep! Don't tell me – you were fighting off that saltie again.'

This was so close to the truth that Sam winced. 'Did you have another visit from Uncle Onay?' he asked.

Lola nodded. 'I'll tell you later. Do you think we can trust these people? This princess, or Birdie, or whatever their names are?'

'I think so,' he said, pushing the bathroom door open. 'Sparrow helped when I was seasick and the princess stopped the Collector sacking me. Anyway, they're the only people I know who might get me into the Octopus.'

Lola sniffed. 'I smell toast. At least they have food. Hurry up in there, I'm *starving*.'

They followed the passage into the main bungalow, with its polished floors and rattan furniture. The room was empty but they heard voices and a promising clink of tableware from the verandah.

Sam opened the screen doors to see Sparrow and the princess dressed in loose cotton pyjamas and sipping coffee. Suka dived for a crust and glided off into the garden.

'Come on, you two must be famished!' the princess smiled.

Sparrow was pouring mugs of a steaming brown drink that didn't smell like coffee. 'Cocoa!' she told Sam as she passed him a basket of thick-sliced toast and a dish of pale butter. 'It's good – try it! We'll talk while you eat.'

Sam took a sip of creamy sweetness. It was the most delicious thing he'd ever tasted.

'I'm confused about *everything*!' Lola took a bite of toast.

'Princess – don't you think—' the princess answered.

'Wait!' Lola interrupted, her mouth full. She pointed at her. 'I thought *you* were the princess?'

Sam looked from one to the other. The young lady who'd just spoken was the princess on the boat. Her skin was paler and her dark hair curled about her face. Sparrow's skin was brown, her nose turned up at the tip. She winked at Sam.

'You do look alike!' he said wonderingly. 'Are you *both* princesses?'

'Sort of – we're cousins!' Sparrow announced. 'But I'm *officially* the Princess of Moonlally. The queen's my mother. I don't enjoy the dressing-up-and-acting-polite stuff that goes with being a princess, so Cousin Ophelia helps me out.'

'I do help, though I usually regret it.' Ophelia rolled her eyes at Sam and Lola.

'But why were you dressed like a man – in a turban?' Sam asked Sparrow.

'Well, outside Moonlally people disapprove of young women travelling alone. If I pretend to be the servant, no one bothers us. So, tell us, Sam Singh and Lola, how did you end up on that road, far from anywhere?'

Lola and Sam exchanged glances.

'Before we tell you, I must send the governor an urgent message,' Lola said. 'The Collect— I mean, Professor Bogusz, his boat was carried out to sea in the storm. The governor needs to set up a search party.'

The princess's cousin – Ophelia – pushed her chair back from the table. 'I'll do that straight away. Do you think he's still at sea?'

'Either that or the pirates have got him,' Lola sniffed. 'I tried to warn him.'

'If the Jalai Rajah's men have taken him captive, they'll demand a hefty ransom,' Sparrow put in. Sam was not used to thinking of her as a princess. Now he could tell Moon he'd eaten breakfast with the Princess of Moonlally.

'Remind me who the Jalai Rajah is again?' he asked.

'King of the sea pirates,' Lola explained. 'That's why no one sails – or treks to the north. It belongs to him.'

'And he's as cut-throat and fearsome as pirates in stories, according to the governor,' Sparrow added. 'I didn't like that man – Professor Bogusz – but even he doesn't deserve to fall into their hands. Now – ' she refilled their mugs with hot cocoa – 'let's hear *your* story. What happened after I saw you both at the Governor's Residence?'

Ophelia hurried back on to the verandah. 'I was so angry at that professor – poking you with his horrible callipers! I've sent a message to the governor, though I'm not sure he deserves rescuing. Go on!'

Sam told of their journey to Lola's village, fumbling for the right words and jumbling parts up. He'd never had a conversation with a princess before, and he felt nervous, unlike Lola, who didn't seem at all shy. But when he looked over for help, she was absorbed in pouring her third mug of cocoa.

'When you asked what was inside his case of specimens, I got curious,' he said. 'That's how I realised the Collector had stolen Uncle Onay to add to his collection of skulls! Lola – have I left anything out?' he asked.

Lola sighed. 'Only the most important part, Sam *Singh*! The glass bottle – with the message from your brother?'

Sam cleared his throat nervously and explained how his fears that Moon was in the Octopus had been confirmed. 'I hoped – because you visit the prison – you might take a message? So he doesn't think I've forgotten him? Please!'

Silence fell. Sam looked down at his plate, heat flaming his face. Had he been foolish to think they'd help him – even if Moon was named after Moonlally? Wealthy people, *important* people like Princess Sparrow and her cousin did not care what happened to those like him – let alone to thieves like Moon.

'By the Lady!' Sparrow shook her head. 'That's quite the voyage, Sam Singh – sailing to the Isle in the hope of finding your brother. *Of course* we'll take him a message. But first—'

Their heads turned as they heard the deep growl of an engine. Lola and Sam stared at the grand, gleaming black car belonging to the governor, now pulling up in front of the verandah. Ophelia hurried to greet the unexpected visitor while Princess Sparrow, Sam noticed, vanished into the bungalow.

The driver stepped out, giving Sam and Lola a curious glance, before bowing to Ophelia, and holding out an envelope in his white-gloved hand.

'A message from the governor, Your Highness.'

Ophelia read the note and looked between Sam and Lola. 'The governor wants to speak with you. He needs more details of where Professor Bogusz disappeared – he's sending the lifeboat.'

Lola nodded. 'I'll go,' she told Ophelia firmly. 'I remember exactly where it was – Sam doesn't know the Isle like I do.' She looked at him. 'Stay here if you want, Sam?'

He shook his head. 'No, I'll come.' He didn't like the Collector, but he owed him. After all, if it wasn't for him, Sam would never have come here to find Moon.

Suka flew down to perch on his shoulder as he stepped outside. Lola was already climbing into the car. He turned to Ophelia and Princess Sparrow, who had reappeared, complete with yellow turban and neat moustache.

'Thank you – for breakfast and everything.'

'This isn't *goodbye*, Sam Singh!' Sparrow winked. 'We have more to discuss. Would you both come back and stay after you've spoken to the governor?'

'I'd like that,' he said, wondering how her moustache worked. Was it stuck on? It did appear a little crooked, now he looked closer.

She added in a whisper. 'Sam, I'll make enquiries about your brother. We're dining at the Residence this evening – it's the governor's annual ball. I should have news for you by then!'

Seventeen

Lola was silent in the car, a frown on her face, as if she was trying to work something out. She had a large canvas bag on her lap.

Sam nudged her. 'Is that *him*?' he whispered, wondering what Lola had seen in her dreams last night. 'Is that your Uncle Onay?'

She nodded, placing a warning finger on her lips. Sam realised he hadn't told the others about her dreams, or Tuke's journey into the spirit world. But those stories didn't belong to him, only to Lola.

The Governor's Residence was in uproar, with the front door wide open and servants scurrying about. Suka shot off, soaring over the mayhem to perch on the head of Colonel Mayonnaise's statue out front. As they entered the marble-floored hallway, Bela, the housekeeper, came hurrying to meet them.

'He's not free yet,' she said, as they heard shouting from a door marked: GOVERNOR'S OFFICE.

'Send a cable to the family!' they heard the governor bellow. 'Are you sure he doesn't have one?'

'He wanted to speak to you before he sends the lifeboat out,' the housekeeper told them. 'But it's a good thing he's busy – look at the state of you! What have you two been doing, wrestling crocodiles? Come and wash first.'

'We washed this morning, Bela!' Lola protested.

The housekeeper ignored her, bustling them through the kitchens. 'That professor would go missing when we're holding the ball this evening. Boffins! There's talk of cancelling the whole thing – and poor Joseph was up half the night baking and icing. Upstairs – I'll find you some clean things.'

She led them up a narrow stairway into her own room, where there was a bathroom with a small, square tub. Sam and Lola had to scrub themselves clean in scalding hot water and soap and pull on the white staff uniforms that Bela laid out for them. These were not designed for children: Sam had to roll his trouser legs up, and Lola was swamped by a dress that reached her ankles.

'We look stupid,' she said gloomily as they studied themselves in the mirror. 'And these clothes are no good for tonight, when—'

Bela burst in and whisked them downstairs. 'Come on – I've a million and one things to do!'

They were led through the grand house, with its silk rugs, china vases and oil paintings, Lola clutching the bag with Uncle Onay inside. Despite his new clothes, Sam felt as out of place as a fly on a white tablecloth. He much preferred Sparrow's comfortable bungalow.

Bela put her ear to the office door. 'Sounds like he's almost finished. You wait here. No sneaking off to climb a tree, Miss Lola, I know your antics. I must check the chandeliers in the ballroom haven't blown a bulb!' and she hurried away.

They could hear the governor muttering through the closed door. 'Pesky piraticals! Can't leave that dried-up old stick to perish, can we?'

'What's going on tonight?' Sam whispered to Lola.

'What?'

'You said these clothes are no good for tonight…' He tugged at the uniform trousers, which flapped around his skinny legs.

Lola nodded. 'I've worked it all out, don't worry. You left the skulls of those poor people in the folly on the lake, right? Tonight, Sam Singh, we'll row out there and rescue them!'

Sam blinked. 'Rescue them! Why? How?'

'Uncle Onay visited me in my dreams again and told me to get them out. Tuke's on his way – he'll do a ceremony to set their spirits free – or else, they'll curse the Isle for ever more – like old Mayo!' She gestured dramatically towards the oil painting.

Sam frowned. 'How are we going to do that without getting caught?'

'During the ball, silly! Everyone's going to be busy dancing and drinking that bubbly wine. They won't notice us.'

'But – we don't have the key to the folly!'

Lola patted her pocket. 'Bela does. Or did. I nabbed it while you were in the bath. I used to play out there all the time when I was little, so I knew which it was.'

'But – what will Tuke do with the skulls? After he's released their spirits, I mean – will he bury them?'

'He'll float them out to sea on a raft – a sea burial.'

'But – how do we build a raft strong enough? That case is heavy.'

Lola flapped her hand open and shut. 'But, but, but... Is that all you can say, Sam Singh? In our village even children know how to build a bamboo raft!'

Sam tried to silence his objections but his mind was brimming. It reminded him of when Moon discussed his pilfering plans. Sam's job was to ask questions. *What if the cook wakes up? What if the cowshed roof gives way?* It was how he was made.

Lola clicked her teeth scornfully. 'If I hadn't seen you stab a crocodile in the eye, I'd say you were *scared*.'

He was about to argue back when the door swung open.

'Lola, my dear. And parrot boy – Sammy, isn't it? Come in, come in!' The governor was squeezed into a tight-fitting red tailcoat and a starched, ruffled shirt tied with a floppy bow. His great belly bulged over black breeches, which ended in white stockings, held up with red satin garters. Exactly the outfit Colonel Mayo wore in the painting, Sam realised, only without the powdered wig.

Lola did the talking. She described the crocodile attack, miming Sam stabbing the beast in the eye with blood-curdling sound effects. Sam began to think he'd done something special after all.

'Now where is this beach? Show me – as accurately as possible!' The governor unrolled a large map on the desk.

Sam leaned forward to examine it. There was the port, with its jumbled streets, and a black circle for the Octopus, labelled: *Prison*. The river they'd travelled up was a blue line meandering over the plateau, marked: *Native Territory*.

Lola's finger came down with a jab. 'There! See that inlet? *That's* where Sam saved me and where the Collector drifted out to sea.'

The inlet was also where the shiny, mechanical vessel had appeared in the water. Sam had never seen a boat like it. What *was* it? Should he tell the governor? He tried to focus on the conversation.

'Hmm!' The governor shook his head so vigorously his jowls wobbled. 'His canoe won't overturn. Your people make sturdy crafts, but with the current, he's bound to have drifted north. We know what *that* means!'

'The Jalai Rajah and his band of dastardly pirates,' Lola put in. 'I did *try* to warn the Collect— the professor, but he wouldn't listen.'

'Those roguish buccaneers demand a hefty ransom! I'll need to send a cable to the mainland and fill out reams of paperwork to get the funds.' The man sank his face into his hands. 'I've heard

GITA RALLEIGH

that if you refuse, they send their victim back in pieces, a finger, then an ear.' He shook his head. 'Enough to put one off the suckling pig, eh? Talking of which, do ask Joseph for some supper before the ball tonight.'

'We will, thank you, Governor.' Lola bobbed a curtsey. 'Come on, Sam!'

128

Eighteen

L ola cajoled the cook into giving them a generous meal of roast chicken sandwiches, pomegranate jellies that hadn't set and two slices of slightly burned fruitcake.

'Keep those uniforms clean, you two,' Joseph warned, as he handed them the tray. 'Bela didn't give you them for nothing, you know. She might need help this evening. The governor's ball is the biggest event of the year.'

Lola led Sam into the grounds, aiming for her favourite tree, the flowering paulownia. Sam whistled for Suka, who glided down gracefully and plucked a raisin from the fruitcake.

'Should we stay near the house?' he asked. 'In case Bela needs us?'

'Don't be silly. If we're too far away to hear Bela call, we can't help, can we?' Lola flopped on the grass, sparing no thought for her white dress. 'As soon as we've eaten, we'll climb the tree. You can see right into the ballroom windows from the top. Once the dancing begins, we'll row out to the folly.' She took a huge bite of her chicken sandwich.

'But…' Sam's belly felt tight and anxious. Sparrow had promised him news of Moon – how would she find them if they were so far away?

Lola took another huge mouthful. 'This is delicious. Can I eat yours if you don't want it?'

Sam handed it to her. There were more holes in Lola's plan than a fishing net! But if she wouldn't listen to him, he'd have to go along with her and steal the Collector's skulls. If they were quick, he might be back in time to catch Sparrow.

From the wide branches of the paulownia, they had an excellent view of the Residence. It was lit up like a bride's house on her wedding day, every window gleaming gold. Inside the ballroom, the governor's guests stood talking and sipping drinks. They waited, until at last they heard the strains of music and the guests began whirling about, even the governor, who was surprisingly nimble for such a large man.

'Look – they're dancing!' Sam said. 'Let's go.'

'You don't think we should wait a bit? That wine with bubbles makes them very silly.'

Sam shook his head. He wanted to get this over with.

'Are we taking Uncle Onay too?' he asked, surprised to see Lola cradle the skull in front of her.

'Of course! He needs to be there. He'll ask the spirits for permission.'

They slid from the tree and tiptoed across the lawn, keeping to the bushes. Lola was right about the uniforms, the stark white stood out in the moonless night, making it difficult to hide. Away from the light and music spilling out from the Residence, the grounds were eerily dark and silent. A loud croaking by the lake made Sam jump.

'Only a night heron,' he said, watching the bird flap away. They found the boat still tied to its post. Sam rowed them across the lake towards the folly, Suka perched on his shoulder. It was so quiet he could hear the splash of his paddles.

Lola remained silent, handing him Bela's key as they approached. The wooden door was stiff, and the key took an effort to turn in the padlock. Sam pushed until it gave, swinging open so they stumbled into darkness.

'We should have brought a candle,' Sam peered into the gloom to see Lola already kneeling before the huge case. She placed Uncle Onay gently beside her, chanting softly in her own language, and took up a rattle, made from pierced shells on a wooden stick. Her eyes closed, she swayed from side to side, shaking it.

Sam walked to the door, thinking he'd keep lookout. But the Residence's brightly lit windows were barely visible through the trees. Lola was right, everyone was too busy to come looking for them.

He heard a sudden clatter, followed by a thud. Lola had slumped to the floor, the rattle fallen from her hand.

'*Lola!*' Sam gulped, hurrying over. 'Lola, what's wrong?'

Outside, a sudden gust of wind made the wooden walls shudder. Clouds shifted and a shaft of moonlight slanted across the floor. Lola lay unconscious, like Tuke on his spirit journey at the village.

'Come back, Lola!' Sam patted her cheek, trying to remember what she'd told him that night. The drum – hadn't she said it was important? Like a kite string, tethering Tuke's spirit to the earth. But there was no drum here, only – the rattle! He grabbed it, jiggling it loudly by her ear.

Suka flew in and landed on Sam's shoulder.

'Suka, help!' he pleaded. 'Lola won't wake up!' He cradled her head carefully in one arm, shaking the rattle with the other. She was warm and breathing – but it was dangerous for her to stay like this too long.

'*Wake up, Lola! Reveillez-vouz! Utho!*' Suka landed on Lola's head and dug his claws in.

'Be careful,' he told the parrot.

'*Ow!* That hurts!' Lola opened her eyes.

'Are you all right? Sorry – I was worried. I asked Suka to wake you.'

Lola rubbed her head and yawned. 'The spirits spoke,' she murmured. 'I told them we're on their side.'

Sam helped her sit up. He wished Lola had warned him. It had been frightening to see her enter a trance. He wanted suddenly to be back by the Residence, music and lively voices drifting from its windows.

'Did it work? Can we go?'

Lola nodded, sleepily. 'They had more to say. But we can move them now.'

'Quick, before anyone finds us. Suka, fly out and check no one's around. Call *danger* if you spot anyone.'

'*Danger! Khatra!*' Suka crowed as he took off.

A half-moon appeared from behind the clouds, reflecting palely on the water. Sam was grateful for its light as he helped a drowsy Lola clamber into the rowboat, then staggered back with the case of skulls, loading it between the thwarts. He remembered to lock the folly, hoping no one would look inside. Suka circled overhead as he rowed them across the lake.

'Lola – should I get help? I was worried when you passed out in there!'

Lola shook her head, but even in the moonlight, Sam saw her lips were pinched and her skin grey. She clutched Uncle Onay to her, shivering.

'It's just – I haven't done that alone before. Tuke's always been with me.'

Sam tied the rowboat firmly to its post and heaved the case on to the bank.

'*Stranger! Ajnabi!*' squawked Suka. He froze, listening for footsteps. What would he do if someone spotted them now? Sam panicked. For a moment, he thought of pushing the case into the water. He helped Lola out of the boat and sat her on top, hoping no one would notice it belonged to the Collector.

'Who's there?' he called.

'Is that you, Sam? It's me – Sparrow!' A slight figure wearing a yellow turban walked across the lawn towards them. 'I've been looking everywhere for you!'

'*Sam! Lo-la!*' They heard Bela's voice from afar. 'Where have those rascals got to? Here I am, run off my feet—'

'Can I ask what you're up to?' Sparrow looked puzzled.

'I'll explain later,' Sam whispered. 'But I'm worried about Lola – she fainted. And we need to hide this – it belongs to the Collector.'

Sparrow scratched her chin. 'Bela's not happy. Let's stash that big case in the car. Lola, can you walk that far?"

Sam and Sparrow struggled along with the case hoisted between them and Lola stumbling behind.

'It's parked over there, the one flying the green orchid flag from its bonnet. Can you manage, Sam? I'll head Bela off.' Sparrow hurried towards the servants' entrance.

Sam heaved the case into the trunk and turned to find Lola slumped on the ground.

'Lola! Here, inside. Lie down.' Sam leaped to open the door and help her in, his mind whirring. What had gone wrong on her visit to the spirit world?

Lola lay along the back seat, pulling the blanket over her with a sigh.

'Was it the spirits?' Sam asked urgently. 'The skulls in the case? Did talking to them make you ill?'

Lola nodded, her eyes closed. 'Spirits,' she murmured. 'So many, Sam! From all over the world…' She flung an arm out sideways.

'We're back! Bela only wanted to give back your clothes – what's going on?'

Sam turned, relieved to see Sparrow returning with Ophelia. He explained quickly, while Ophelia felt Lola's pulse at her wrist.

'Has she eaten anything?'

'Yes, loads. I think—'

'Roast chicken sandwiches!' Lola whispered. 'Fruit cake.' She licked her lips.

'Hmm. She seems a little better. Let's get her home and send for a doctor in the morning,' Ophelia decided.

'I take it that big case in the trunk is Professor Bogusz's grisly collection of skulls?' Sparrow asked.

'*What!*' Ophelia squeaked. 'You haven't brought them here? That man and his crackpot theories.'

'Um, Lola's grandfather is coming to bless them… or something?' Sam was convinced that talking to the spirits had made Lola ill. A doctor couldn't fix that. They needed Tuke. He wondered how to explain this to Ophelia, as they piled into the car and drove off.

'Old Mayo's riding again...' Lola murmured. Hooves clattered behind them as they trundled up the long drive towards the Residence gates.

Sam turned to peer through the rear window and was startled out of his skin. A white shape materialised from the trees – a great marble horse and rider, cantering with a wild stomping of hooves.

The ghostly rider galloped up the drive, gaining on them effortlessly, until he was level with the car. Petrified, Sam stared at the horseman's moving mouth, while his rasping voice buzzed in his ears, coming from all directions at once. Sam couldn't be entirely sure what he said, but it sounded like *freedom*. At last, they were through the gates, leaving the apparition behind. Sam slumped back on the seat, dazed. He had just seen his first ghost.

Nineteen

Sam woke late. He hadn't been able to fall asleep the night before, anxious about Lola. But now her bunk was empty, and he was relieved to see her on the sunny verandah, drinking a tall glass of coconut water and looking much perkier. Suka flew down and pecked him gently on the earlobe.

'Ouch! Morning, boy.'

'Come and drink this, Sam. You look washed out,' Ophelia tutted as she poured him a glass. 'I'll ask the doctor to look at you when he comes for Lola.'

'No need,' Lola said firmly. 'I'm all better, thank you. I had a good night's sleep. Only I'm famished!'

'That's lucky. I've made a special Moonlally breakfast!' Sparrow proclaimed.

Sam was astonished to see her carrying in a huge platter of spicy potato cakes, and a bowl of plantain jam, a striped apron tied over the same simple white tunic and trousers as Ophelia. He hadn't thought a *princess* would do the cooking herself.

'My grandmother's recipe!' she said. 'Eat up, both of you.'

But Sam couldn't eat – not without news of Moon. All the commotion last night meant he hadn't asked about his brother. Time was running out before the *Yellow Pearl* sailed – by his count, last night had been his fourth on the Isle. He needed Sparrow and Ophelia's help.

Before he opened his mouth, Sparrow spoke, her tone serious. 'Sam, Lola – we're on the same side, so I think it's time to be honest with each other.' She poured herself coffee and silence fell over the table.

Sam and Lola exchanged glances. But Sparrow wasn't talking to them.

'I *knew* you'd tell all, Mignon,' Ophelia sighed. 'I warn you, the less they know, the safer they are! But do as you please. As usual.' She leaned forward to press the back of her hand to Lola's forehead. 'No temperature.'

Lola twisted away and pointed at Sparrow. 'Wait – why did you call her *Mignon?* How many names do you people have?'

Sparrow grinned. 'Mignon's my real name. But only Ophelia and my mother call me that. To everyone else, I'm Sparrow.'

'If we're *confessing*, I want to know why these two stole that ghastly collection of skulls!' Ophelia huffed. 'What are we to do with them?'

'Tell them, Lola?' Sam nudged her. 'About what Onay said in your dream—'

'That was *delicious*.' Lola wiped her mouth with a napkin and waved it in the air. 'Nothing for you to worry about. Sam and I rescued those people, so Tuke – my grandfather – can set their spirits free.'

'That's wonderful of him,' Sparrow said gravely, giving Ophelia a warning glance.

'But why?' Ophelia put in. 'I mean, it *is* kind. But they're not *your* ancestors!'

Lola shook her head. 'They've been taken by the Collector on his travels. And they're *furious* about it. Tuke must release their spirits over water, so they're free to travel home. Or they'll curse the Isle for ever.' She sighed. 'Strangers! Nothing but trouble for our people.'

'But couldn't we send them back to the places they've been taken from?' Ophelia objected.

Lola nodded. 'That would be best,' she agreed. 'If we knew where in the world that was.'

'Aren't there labels identifying them?'

Sam shook his head slowly. 'Only numbers in black ink.'

Lola sat back in her chair and sighed. 'Now tell us – what are *you* hiding?'

'Well…' Sparrow reached under the table and took out a scroll of paper, sweeping the dishes aside to unroll it. 'Always wanted to do that!' she said, winking at Sam. 'You'll be interested in this.'

They craned forward to look. 'What is it – a map?' Lola asked.

But this was nothing like the map the governor had shown them the day before. It was the plan of a building in blue ink, with a circular tower at the centre and slender wings stretching outwards. Sam counted them. There were eight.

'It's the *Octopus*! Is this to do with Moon? You said you'd ask about him at the jail.'

Sparrow looked up. 'We did ask, Sam. But your brother's not on the list of inmates.'

'That means he's escaped!' Sam leaped to his feet, hope bounding into his heart. 'I know he was planning to – he said so in that message in the glass bottle.'

Sparrow gave him a gentle smile. 'You might be right, Sam. This plan is from an ex-inmate, who traded it with a pirate.'

'But you came here to inspect the Octopus. Why wouldn't they just *give* you a plan?' Lola asked.

Sparrow made a face. 'Officially we're inspecting the prison. That isn't the whole truth. One of our friends is inside.'

'So, you're here to visit them?' Lola concluded. 'Like Sam Singh and his brother.'

'*Sam Singh!*' Suka echoed from the garden. '*Moon Singh!*'

Sam studied the blue-inked plan closely. A double line in red caught his eye. It led from the furthest tip of one tentacle, past a boundary labelled 'electric fence' all the way to the sea wall. He tapped it with his finger.

'This line – there's a tunnel – or escape route marked here!' He stared at Sparrow and Ophelia. 'You're not visiting this friend – you're going to break them out!'

'What?' Lola jumped, elbowing the dish of plantain jam which landed on the terrace floor with a crash. 'That's impossible!'

Suka swooped down, crying, '*Jam, confiture, chutney!*' tailed by a troop of jungle crows, cawing *jam*. The hungry flock scuffled and pecked in a noisy ruckus until they were shooed away by Ophelia.

'I didn't think—' Sam and Lola spoke at the same time.

Sparrow laughed. 'What didn't you think?'

'I didn't think a *princess* would break someone out of jail,' Sam said.

'I didn't think crows could talk!' Lola picked up a shining black feather one of the crows had left and stuck it in her hair.

'It did sound like they were crowing *jam*!' Sparrow agreed. 'Suka's more of a professor than the professor himself.'

'Your friend…' Sam hesitated. It was not polite to ask this question among the land pirates, but he was sure Sparrow wouldn't mind. 'What did he *do*, exactly?'

Sparrow smiled. 'Jay? He did nothing wrong, I promise!'

Ophelia sat forward. 'We need to explain about Moonlally. We're different from the rest of Indica – the mainland,' she added for Lola's benefit.

'We're a queendom, for one thing,' Sparrow put in. 'Much of Indica is colonised by people from Europa, like the Isle. Moonlally's altogether different – it's an independent state.'

'With a free press,' Ophelia continued. 'And voting rights for all.'

'What's that got to do with your friend ending up in the Octopus?' Sam was puzzled.

'Ophelia, Jay and I worked together to restore the queendom,' Sparrow told them. 'But our ideas aren't popular outside Moonlally – in fact, they're banned.'

'Jay's a hothead. His newspaper, *The Revolutionary Rag,* spreads rebellion to all Indica,' Ophelia added. 'He was caught with a bundle of contraband papers in Samudra—'

'—and transported to the Isle of Lost Voices,' Sparrow concluded. 'Sentenced to ten years of hard labour.'

Ophelia shook her head. 'We couldn't leave him here. It's been six months!'

'Jay's letters – in code, of course – hinted at a tunnel to the sea wall.' Sparrow tapped the paper, now stained with coffee and plantain jam. 'We got hold of this plan – his cell's at the tip of that tentacle. We're going to pick him up on the other side of the wall.'

'What about the watchtower?' Lola objected. 'At night, that revolving light shines into every cell. They'll see your friend's missing and by the time he's out of the tunnel, the alarm will sound. Any boats on the water will be spotted by the guards.'

'But we're not going to be spotted. We'll be travelling underwater,' Sparrow explained. 'We have a special type of boat – a submersible!'

Sam, swigging coconut water, spluttered and coughed. He'd watched the silver machine surface from the waves, and now he knew what it was! Lola slapped him on the back.

'I – I saw it – the submersible!' Sam croaked, wiping his mouth on his sleeve. 'I thought it was a whale ship – it looked like a mechanical fish.'

Sparrow grinned. 'Careless of our pilot to let you see him. It does look a bit like a whale or a fish, but it's a sea-going craft that travels underwater.'

'It's stationed just off the Isle,' Ophelia added. 'We call it the *Dugong*.'

# Twenty

'We know the floodlight on top of the Octopus takes three minutes to circle.' Ophelia turned the teapot lid slowly. 'If Jay enters the tunnel as soon as it's gone past—'

The four of them were going over the escape plan, using a teapot for the Octopus, forks for its eight wings and a salt cellar on its side for the *Dugong*.

'First, he'll unblock the tunnel entrance,' Sparrow pointed out, walking her fingers along a fork. 'And then it's 300 metres between Jay's cell and the sea wall. We don't know how wide the tunnel is – he might have to crawl on his belly.'

Sam chugged the salt cellar along the table, leaving a trail of white crystals. 'How fast is the *Dugong*?' he asked.

'Speed of 5-7 knots. It has enough air to stay submerged for fifteen minutes without breaching,' Sparrow told him.

Ophelia frowned. 'That means we'll only be a few kilometres from shore before the *Dugong* needs to surface,' she pointed out. 'The guards might spot us.'

'True,' Sparrow agreed gloomily. 'We need to delay the guards sounding the alarm until we're further away.'

'Well, we're seeing Jay in prison today,' Ophelia reminded her. 'To finalise the time of the escape – that might give us an idea?'

'*Friend! Ami! Dost! Nanban! Milale!*' Suka squawked from the garden.

'Who's that?' Sparrow snatched up the plan and sprang to her feet, alarmed. 'I'd better hide this.' Her words were followed by the clattering of Tuke's hand drum.

'Don't worry,' Lola joined in, rapping on the table. 'That sounds like my grandfather.'

They found the old man kneeling by the car, rattling his drum and chanting in a low voice. He was dressed in travelling clothes: a ragged vest with a red cloth knotted round his waist and a hemp bag hung across his back. His grass skirt, palm-leaf headdress and clay tribal markings were gone, but he was just as impressive. Sam waited for Lola to greet her grandfather, then stepped forward to grasp his shoulders and bump foreheads. Sparrow and Ophelia folded their hands in a namaste.

'Welcome, sir. Would your grandfather like breakfast?' Ophelia asked Lola.

Lola spoke to Tuke and shook her head. 'Tuke's not happy to see those people locked in the trunk. First, we need to lay them out in the garden and fill them with flowers and special herbs. After that, he'll build a bamboo raft for the ceremony.'

'Of course. But do offer him a cool drink first. He's had a long journey. We'll help with the arrangements,' Ophelia urged her.

Tuke sat on the verandah steps drinking coconut water, Suka perched on his knee, while Lola brought him up to date.

'Perhaps I should stay and help?' Sparrow asked. 'It sounds as if there's a lot to be done.'

Ophelia gave her a look. 'Mignon, you go. *I'll* stay,' she said firmly. 'You must see Jay. Wear my lace sari and cover your face, no one will know.'

Sparrow's face clouded. 'Visit Jay on my own – in that awful place?'

'I'll come with you,' Sam offered. He wanted to see it for himself – the Octopus jail his brother had feared so much. And now he knew that Moon had been inside, he might find a clue to his escape.

'I'll help Tuke. Ophelia can give us what we need,' Lola told him.

'That makes sense,' Ophelia agreed. 'Sam, why don't you wear Sparrow's turban and mooch and go along as her servant? You're almost the same height.'

Sparrow helped him bind the yellow turban and stick on the false moustache. 'I know it's itchy, but don't scratch!' she warned. 'We can't have it falling off.'

She disappeared, emerging minutes later dressed in the lace sari Ophelia had worn on the *Yellow Pearl* and looking the picture of a princess.

'*Sam Singh?*' Suka flew down, squawking his surprise at Sam's appearance.

'Stay here, boy. Prison's no place for a parrot,' Sam told him, gently stroking his neck.

They set off, Sparrow steering the car skilfully down the hilly slope, past the huddled buildings of the port and towards the towering Octopus.

'I warn you, Sam, this prison's a pretty grim place,' she told him. 'You'll have to be strong. I know it's hard to think of your brother in there.'

Sam nodded. 'What did they say about him?'

'Only that they had no inmate named Moon or Moonlally Singh. Did he have distinguishing marks – birthmarks or tattoos?'

'Yes!' Sam rolled up his sleeve and showed her. 'He's got a scorpion tattooed on his left arm – like this. All the boys of our tribe have one.' It was hard to believe it was days since he'd crossed the black water to the Isle. His old life as a land pirate felt very far away.

Sparrow nodded. 'The superintendent's not a pleasant man, but I'll try.'

'Can I ask you something, Princess?'

'Of course! But call me Sparrow.'

'Well – you said your friend's only been inside six months but he's dug a tunnel out of the Octopus? That doesn't sound right.' Sam had heard many stories of jail escapes – digging a tunnel was slow, tedious work.

'Why not?'

'Even with proper equipment, a tunnel takes *ages*. In prison, you're lucky to have an old spoon to dig with!'

Sparrow closed her eyes. The car swerved and Sam grabbed the dashboard. She opened them again, steadied the wheel and recited:

For you, I'd burrow like a hare.
Like a deer, for you I'd flee.
From citadel to boundless sea,
where I'd take the air with thee.

Sam's confusion must have shown because Sparrow burst out laughing.

'Sam, your expression! I'm sorry, you must think I'm loopy. That's how we knew they were coded messages – the poems Jay wrote in his letters. Jay *hates* poetry!'

'Are you saying – that *poem* told you about the tunnel?'

'Yes – burrow like a hare, see! There were lots of others – let me think.' She cleared her throat.

If you and I could sail the seas
And lift our voices on the breeze.
My heart would know but one song:
O Mignon, Mignon, my Mignon.

Sparrow made a noise as if she was being sick. But Sam saw she was blushing. 'You see? We gathered there was a tunnel from Jay's poems – all that stuff about the sea meant he needed a boat to escape.'

'Er, I don't think I do…' To Sam the poems sounded like nonsense. Had Sparrow and Ophelia built a whole jailbreak around such thin evidence?

Sparrow laughed again. 'Poor Sam – stuck with us. Don't worry, we didn't plan this escapade on poetry alone! Like I said, we checked the jail records. Jay's cell is closest to the sea. And our *Dugong* pilot has found the opening in the sea wall. It's barely visible at low tide and covered with seaweed.'

'An opening to a tunnel?'

'To a disused sewage pipe. Those red lines on that plan I showed you. We think the tunnel from Jay's cell connects to it.'

Sam thought about this. Escaping through a disused sewage pipe sounded like one of Moon's schemes. 'Someone else might have tunnelled from the cell to the pipe?'

'I see what you're getting at, Sam. Let me pull over, we're almost there.' Sparrow steered the car slowly on to the grassy bank. 'There it is,' she nodded grimly.

Ahead, the black tower of the Octopus loomed, its round windows observing their approach. The floodlight on its domed roof reminded Sam of the *kepi* hats policemen wore on the mainland. It was forbidding, enclosed by a high wire fence, the gates flanked by guards. The electric fence, Sam remembered, from the plan.

Sparrow took off her glasses. 'Sam, do you think your brother dug that tunnel?'

'Moon's the king of prison escapes. He once fled a police cell by shimmying right under the bars.'

He frowned. 'Do you still have Jay's letters? Did they say anything else?'

'They're back in Moonlally. But I memorised all his poems. You know there *was* one about the moon.'

Condemned alone to this cell.
I have a friend though none can tell.
His silver beams do light my way,
From lonely night to bright new day.

She looked at him, her eyes shining. 'By the Lady – I think you're right, Sam. Moon dug that tunnel – and escaped! But the superintendent's a tricky man – we can't ask too many questions.'

Sam nodded. 'I'll leave that to you. What do I call you in there – Princess?'

'Your Highness, officially.' She smiled at him and slid her glasses back on. 'I'm glad you're with me, Sam. I'd hate to go in there alone.'

The guards were expecting them. They saluted at the green and white Moonlally flag fluttering from the bonnet as the gates swung slowly open.

'The green orchid flag of Moonlally!' Sparrow whispered. 'To think we'd be in prison for flying it a few years ago!' She shook her head.

'I believe this plan's going to work and Jay will be free. I know it sounds reckless, Sam. But reckless ideas have changed Moonlally for the better – and Jay was part of them. That's why we must try and rescue him, however slim the chances.'

Beyond the gates, a long driveway cut straight through the prison's bare and dusty grounds to the high watchtower of the Octopus. Sam stared up at its round windows, flashing menacingly to survey the cell blocks stretching like black tentacles below. Sparrow halted the car before the great iron-clad doors. She drummed her fingers on the dashboard then adjusted her glasses and pulled her lace sari to cover her face.

'Ready, Sam? Whatever the superintendent says, don't let him get to you,' she murmured.

Sam swallowed. He checked his moustache was in place and tightened his turban as Sparrow floated elegantly towards the entrance. He'd never been inside a prison and found it hard to shake the fear he wouldn't be allowed out again.

A bald man with a sweaty face greeted them with a mock bow. 'If it isn't Her *Highness*,' he drawled with an unpleasant smirk. 'Can't get enough of us, can you? And who's this? You're not taking the boy inside?'

'I am, Superintendent. Thank you.' Sparrow spoke as if her teeth were pressed tightly together. 'We sail on the *Yellow Pearl* tomorrow. This is my final visit. I shan't take up much of your time.'

Twenty-one

'Better give the jail committee a good report, Your Highness.' The superintendent's laugh made Sam feel as if a spider had scuttled down his back.

He stared at the cell blocks, their rows of iron-barred doors, each facing the blank wall of the next block. He couldn't imagine his brother confined to such cramped conditions. Now he understood what Tuke had meant. No wonder Moon's spirit was dim – like a flame without enough air to burn.

'We'll see, Superintendent,' Sparrow replied as they headed into the central tower. 'The governor has granted permission for me to speak to one of my countrymen today.'

'Category D, isn't he? You can expect a guard close at hand during your visit.'

'Naturally, Superintendent. What does the D stand for?'

'D stands for *dangerous*. Seditionists, mutineers and revolutionaries! Horrible lot. Give me an honest thief or murderer any day.'

'I'm grateful, Superintendent. It's the plight of these political prisoners – or freedom fighters as they call themselves – that concerns us.'

'Freedom fighters – *pah!* Hang 'em all if I could,' the superintendent spat. 'You'll see him in my office.'

They climbed a narrow, twisting flight of stairs, coming out into a round room with a curved ceiling and eight circular windows. The place was sparsely furnished; a mahogany desk, an empty bookcase and a moth-eaten tiger skin rug in the centre. Sam realised they were at the top of the Octopus; only the white floodlight was above them.

'Wait over there, Your Highness.'

Sparrow seated herself behind the desk. 'Oh – another thing. I sent word to ask after a young man but they told me he wasn't on the roll call of inmates. I've since learned he has a distinctive tattoo – a scorpion on his left arm.' She smiled at the superintendent. 'I'm sure you wouldn't forget a prisoner like that – would you?'

The superintendent looked embarrassed. 'We did have one rascal with such a tattoo.' He cleared his throat. 'He attempted escape over the sea wall in a fishing boat.'

'Escape, really? But I thought escaping the Octopus was impossible?'

The man's face turned red. '*Attempted* escape, I said, with two other conspirators. Their boat overturned with no survivors.'

'I'm sorry to hear that, Superintendent. Did you find their bodies?'

'Didn't bother.' The man sniffed. 'Saved us burying them. Right, I'll get your category D.'

Sam gripped the hard edge of the desk. Could the superintendent's words be true? Had Moon drowned? He wanted to howl.

'Are you all right, Sam?' Sparrow whispered. 'Take a breath of air at that window. Quick, before he comes back!'

Sam stumbled towards the open window, tears blurring his eyes. Below, a row of cells unfurled towards the sea wall. The walkway along the flat roof was patrolled by guards. It was painful enough to think of his brother locked up. But *drowned*? Moon with his quick, easy laugh. Moon, who'd scale the highest wall, climb the spindliest tree and shoot an arrow to its target from a hundred paces.

Then he remembered, with a rush of relief. Tuke hadn't seen Moon's spirit among the Isle's dead. His brother couldn't be gone. Could he?

Sparrow twisted round in her chair. 'I hear footsteps, Sam—'

Sam hurried back and stood to attention, struggling to quell his feelings and make his face blank. He looked up at the shuffle of footsteps and clank of irons. The prisoner, his hands cuffed in front of him, was brought in. He was tall and skinny, dressed in black prison garb. A spark of recognition flared in his eyes as he glanced at Sparrow, then lowered his gaze.

The guard pushed him roughly into a wooden chair.

Sparrow leaned forward. 'I'm the Princess of Moonlally. So glad to meet you, Mr—'

'No names!' The guard waved his truncheon threateningly as he walked to the door.

The prisoner nodded at a badge pinned to his shirt. 'Pleased to meet you, Your Highness. You can call me D-1567.'

'I've come to ask how you're treated here,' Sparrow spoke loudly, her voice echoing off the bare walls. Then she whispered softly. 'Not long now.'

'Badly, Your Highness,' the prisoner mumbled. 'The rations are disgusting, the work unending and as for the guards—' He glanced at the doorway and stopped.

Sparrow pulled a handkerchief from her pocket and dabbed at her eyes.

'I'm sorry to hear that. We hope our report will lead to an improvement in your conditions.' She glanced at the guard, scratching his behind with his truncheon and spread the handkerchief on to the desk. It was embroidered with a plan of the jail.

'How... much... time?' Sparrow asked as she walked her fingertips delicately from the sewn-on tentacle tip to the sea wall.

'Five...' the prisoner replied. He spread out five fingers of his cuffed right hand.

Five... Sam realised what he meant. It would take him five minutes to crawl through the tunnel to the opening on the sea wall.

'I hope you've enjoyed your stay on the Isle, Your Highness?' the prisoner asked.

'Indeed. The Isle lit by a full moon is a beautiful sight. I've heard the cry of the *Dugong* on its shores.'

'I hope to hear it one day.' They looked at each other in silence. Sparrow tucked the embroidered handkerchief into her pocket.

'You will – tomorrow at midnight!' she whispered. 'That's the signal, we'll be waiting!'

The superintendent entered the room, scowling. 'Time's up, Your Highness,' he bellowed. 'Guard, remove the prisoner!'

The guard walked over, keys jangling at his belt. The prisoner – Jay – was prodded to his feet, lowering his head as he was led away.

'Thank you for the use of your office, Superintendent. Such a magnificent view!' Sparrow rose from her seat.

'I can watch over the whole place from here,' the man grunted. 'Every cell. If I spot trouble, I sound the alarm and then—' The superintendent chuckled softly. 'Then it's the rope for any troublemakers!' He pointed to the nearest window.

Sam shuddered. In a corner of the bleak yard stood the high wooden frame of a gallows. Supposing they caught Jay? Would he hang there, his body swaying helplessly? He swallowed the panic rising within him. Wherever Moon was now, at least his brother's life had not ended in this miserable place.

Twenty-two

S parrow's hands gripped the wheel as she steered the car up the winding road to the hills. Below, Sam could see the white cube of the Governor's Residence, the messy sprawl of the port and further up the coast, the Octopus' menacing black tower. He unwound his turban and peeled off the moustache, relieved to be out of the place.

This was the same route they'd driven up from the river, that night he and Lola returned, only their surroundings had been blanketed in darkness.

'Would you mind if we didn't go straight into the house? I need a moment,' Sparrow began, turning off the engine. They had arrived at the bungalow and were parked just up the hill. Sam could hear Lola's voice carrying from the garden.

'Of course.' He glanced over anxiously to see Sparrow's face wet with tears.

She began to cry, her shoulders racked with sobs. 'It's so hard to see him like that! Almost worse than not seeing him. Thin and sad, his wrists bruised from the shackles.'

Sam patted her arm gently. 'Don't cry, Princess. He'll be free soon, your friend.'

She blew her nose on the embroidered handkerchief. I'm sorry, Sam. Especially as you don't even know where your brother is—'

'I know he's not in the Octopus, at least,' Sam pointed out.

Sparrow sighed. 'True. We'll find him, I promise. Never mind what that superintendent said.'

Sam looked out of the window and down to the shore. The sea was a calm turquoise, foamy waves rolling across the bay. He leaned forward as his eye caught a distant metallic glint in the sunlight.

'What's that – out at sea?'

'By the Lady – the *Dugong*! Well spotted, Sam!' Sparrow took a brass telescope from the glove compartment, swung out of the car and hopped on to the bonnet. Sam followed, scrambling to sit beside her.

'That's cheered me up! How could we possibly fail with our magnificent machine? Take a look.' She showed him how to put his eye to the scope. 'You twist this dial to focus.'

Sam just caught the sleek silver curve of the *Dugong* as it sank beneath the surface.

'Why does it go up and down in the water like that?'

'For air. Shri, our chief engineer, is the most brilliant inventor. There are three problems with underwater travel: air to breathe, how to resist water pressure and the force needed to propel the vehicle forward. The *Dugong* sucks in fresh air and equalises pressure by expelling stale air, which drives the ship onwards.'

'So, it comes up to breathe – like a real dugong?'

'Yes – it's genius! Although it can't go too deep or stay underwater for too long. We have an oxygen supply in case of emergencies. Mostly, the *Dugong* trundles happily 3 to 5 metres below the surface.'

'The *Dugong*'s going to pick up Jay? But you said you're leaving on the *Yellow Pearl* tomorrow...'

'That's for appearances. Everyone – especially the prison officials – must think we've left the Isle before Jay's escape. Once we're at sea, we'll transfer to the submersible, and swoosh back to grab Jay at midnight. The crew of the *Yellow Pearl* will cover for us, it's all arranged. We were planning it the night I found you seasick.'

'And you'll take Jay home to Moonlally?'

Sparrow shook her head sadly. 'He'll be a fugitive from justice. We must smuggle him out of Indica. We're still puzzling over where he might be safe.' She took a deep breath. 'Right. Let's go home. I feel better. Saltwater cures everything, the fisherfolk say – tears, sweat or swimming in the sea.'

The escape plan might involve all three, Sam thought to himself, as they climbed back into the car and eased down the hill, swinging round to halt by the fig tree. An emerald cloud of parrots flocked from its branches, circling overhead with cries of, '*Sam Singh, Sam Singh, Sam Singh.*'

'All these birds – how can you tell which one's Suka?' Sparrow exclaimed. 'I'd better reverse the car out from under the tree. We can't return it to the governor covered in parrot poop!'

Sam turned as the bird landed on his shoulder. 'Suka!' He buried his face in his soft feathers.

'*Sam sad! Dukh! Triste! Thunbam!*' Suka remarked.

'What are you sad about, Sam?' Lola appeared on the verandah.

'I'm all right,' Sam told her. He glanced over to see Sparrow still in the car and lowered his voice. 'But Princess Sparrow was upset to see her friend in prison.'

Ophelia hurried out. 'Did she finalise a time? Perhaps we should go through the plan again. I'll make chai!' She ran back into the bungalow.

'All these people do is drink tea!' Lola screwed up her nose. 'What did you find out about your brother?'

'I think Moon dug the tunnel Jay is using! The prison superintendent said someone with a scorpion tattoo made an escape – the boat sank – but I know he made it.'

'Of course he did! Tuke found his spirit among the living, not the dead.'

'If only I knew where he was…' Sam trailed off.

'You'll find him. You were right about him being imprisoned in the Octopus – and escaping.'

Sam was silent, remembering Lola's words when he'd found Moon's message.

She gave him a wry smile, as if she knew what he was thinking. 'I know I said it was impossible for your brother to survive in the forest. But you know Moon better than anyone else. Anyway, when I said those things, I didn't—' She hesitated.

'Didn't what?'

'I didn't know *you,* Sam Singh. Not like I do now.'

Sam felt his face grow warm. 'How are things here?' he asked quickly.

'We've been busy!' Lola led him into the garden. 'Tuke must be tired out – he's already started on the raft.'

The skulls stolen by the Collector had been arranged on a table, each one decorated with yellow marigold flowers. Small wax candles burned before them. Sam counted twenty-four. Twenty-four human skulls, taken from their own lands and people. Uncle Onay – he presumed it was Onay – had been placed on his own small table facing them, garlanded with a crown of leaves.

Tuke was seated on the grass, binding together wide canes of bamboo. He waved a hand.

'He's been at it all afternoon,' Lola explained. 'Tomorrow, we'll help him finish the raft, then take these people down to the sea for the ceremony.'

Sam nodded. He knew from his own tribe's beliefs that it was necessary to send dead spirits on their way and not let them linger in the world of the living. He wondered what it was like to *see* them, as Lola and Tuke did, feeling an unpleasant shiver run down his neck.

They returned to sit at the table on the verandah with Sparrow, whose eyes, Sam noticed, were red-rimmed.

'Did Jay really look that bad?' Ophelia asked.

'Worse than I imagined,' Sparrow sighed. 'He's very thin. Bruises all down his arms. But we fixed a time – tomorrow at midnight.'

'Let's go through the plan again,' Ophelia unfolded the paper.

'Wait – midnight?' Lola exclaimed. 'Tuke needs to hear this.'

She ran off into the garden and returned to explain. 'Midnight's the time for our ceremony, too. It's full moon tomorrow – when good spirits overpower evil.'

Tuke spoke, leaning forward and stabbing a finger at the plan of the Octopus.

'My grandfather wants us to send them off here, by the sea wall,' she translated. 'There are steps down to the water and a platform to launch the raft.'

'But is that a good idea with Jay's escape?' Ophelia objected. 'Won't Tuke's ceremony attract attention?'

'It might be a useful distraction!' Sparrow pointed out. 'Can you ask your grandfather exactly what happens?'

Lola spoke with Tuke. 'My grandfather will be up on the sea wall, guiding the spirits of these people towards their homes. Sam and I will launch the raft from the bottom of the steps. The spirits will rise over the water in a mist – it'll be a proper fog with so many of them. And as they drift away, the wind will rise.'

'The guards might not spot the *Dugong* if there's a fog,' Sam said.

'And it travels underwater so the wind won't affect it,' Sparrow added.

'We can't rely on weather made by *spirits*!' Ophelia objected. 'We need a diversion inside the Octopus. One to distract the guards from Jay's empty cell!'

Sam didn't doubt the spirits *could* make weather – he'd seen that for himself at Lola's village. The problem was their lack of solidity. They couldn't move things about or make sounds or— 'What about Colonel Mayo?' he said excitedly.

'Who?' Sparrow asked.

'You've seen his statue outside the Residence, Mignon,' Ophelia told her. 'But what can he do? He's been dead for a century!'

'His statue gallops about every night. You can hear its hooves!' Sam gabbled.

Lola clicked her fingers. 'We can ask him! He's not bound to the Residence.' She pointed at Sam. 'I like your idea. If we can get old Mayo to gallop around the prison, shouting, "Treason!" in his croaky old voice, well, that ought to distract the guards.' She leaped to her feet. 'Come on, Sam, we need to talk to him!'

'I heard it as *freedom*,' Sam confessed. 'First time I saw a ghost.' With a shudder, he recalled the statue's creaking voice as they'd driven from the Residence.

'You can't go now – what about supper?' Ophelia threw her hands up. 'I made soup! I chopped vegetables and everything!'

'I'll change into my disguise and run these two down to the Residence to talk to the ghost statue?' Sparrow offered. 'Ophelia *hates* cooking,' she whispered, steering them out of the room. 'You'll do better at the Residence.'

Lola and Tuke exchanged words. 'Tuke says he'll stay and have the vegetable soup. I'm sure it'll be *delicious*,' she added unconvincingly.

Ophelia sighed. 'All right. But don't stay too late – we've a long day tomorrow.'

Suka swooped down to land on Sam's shoulder as they walked out to the verandah. '*Sam Singh?*' he enquired, flexing his claws.

THE VOYAGE OF SAM SINGH

'*Ow!* We're off to the Residence to talk to old Mayo – listen, Suka!' Another idea had come to him. 'The word *freedom*. Can you teach your parrot friends in that tree to say it?'

'*Freedom! Liberté! Azadi! Viduthalai!*'

'You only have to teach them *freedom* – they don't need to know it in every language, Professor Suka,' Lola added.

'*Freedom!*' Suka soared off into the tree. '*Freedom! Freedom!*'

Moments later, the flock rose up to circle above the bungalow, brilliant green against the falling dusk. '*Freedom! Freedom! Freedom!*' came their squawks.

Sam grinned at Lola. If the guards heard shouts of *freedom*, surely *that* would distract them?

'To recap,' Ophelia said, holding open the door of the car, 'at a signal from the *Dugong*, Tuke will release the spirits.' She flourished a hand at the verandah, where the old man stood. 'Then a fog descends, the wind blows and a ghostly horseman gallops about. *Clippety-clop.*'

'*And* the parrots squawk *freedom*!' Lola added.

'And a flock of parrots...' Ophelia raised an eyebrow. 'Is that enough for Jay to escape through the tunnel unnoticed?'

Sam and Lola looked at each other. Ophelia was right – put that way, their plan sounded as substantial as sea mist.

'It's all we have.' Sparrow stuck her moustache on, shrugged and started the car engine. 'By the Lady – it'll have to do!'

Twenty-three

At the Residence, Sparrow accompanied them around the back of the house to the staff entrance.

'You two slip into the kitchens and see if you can nab an early supper from Joseph,' she told them. 'I need to speak to Bela.'

This suited the children, who had noticed a promising scent of baking bread coming from the kitchen door.

Despite his gruff tone, Joseph seemed happy to see them. 'Lola – you again! How did you know I've just taken a tray of rolls out of the oven? Doesn't the princess feed you?'

'Not enough – I'm starving!' Lola told him. 'What's going on, Joseph?'

The cook looked grave. 'Governor's in a right flap about your Professor Bogusz,' he nodded at Sam. 'Barely touched his lunch. Plenty of leftover ham for you two.' The cook lowered his voice. 'I heard the pirates got him? And the Jalai Rajah's demanded fifty gold pieces. Fifty!'

'*Fifty gold sovereigns*? For the Collector – no way is he worth that much,' Lola shook her head.

'What if the governor can't pay?' Sam asked.

Joseph drew a finger across his throat and clicked his tongue. 'Those pirates don't keep their prisoners long. Plenty of water in the ocean, if you get my meaning.'

Sam gulped. He had the uncomfortable feeling he was somehow responsible for the professor. But if he hadn't run back to tell Lola, Uncle Onay would be lost for ever.

'Can we speak to the governor?' he asked. 'Lola and I were the last ones to see him. Maybe we can help?'

Joseph shrugged. 'Eat up and run along to his study. But don't say it was me that told you.'

They ate crusty ham rolls, still warm from the oven and slathered in butter, with pickled carrots on the side. Sam followed Lola through the hallway, glancing at the portrait in its gold frame. He remembered the clatter of ghostly hooves and the unnatural voice he'd heard in their last encounter. Old Mayo sat on a padded throne, straight-backed and glaring into the distance, his red tailcoat tightly buttoned. His face, under the powdered wig, looked pinched and angry. Would his ghost really help them?

The governor's study door stood open and he was grumbling under his breath, '*Tea!* I need tea – ah, Lola my dear! How are you? I was about to send for tea.'

'I'll run to the kitchen and ask Joseph!' Lola said and promptly disappeared, leaving Sam alone with him.

'Come in, Sammy.' The governor beckoned to him. 'Sit yourself down. I don't mind telling you that Professor Bogusz has caused me an infernal amount of bother!'

'Sorry, sir.' Sam sidled in nervously and perched on the slippery edge of a leather armchair. Every object in the room gleamed: the mahogany desk, leather chairs and silver inkstand. This was the first time he'd spoken to the governor without Lola.

'Do you have any idea what those blasted pirates are asking for the professor?' The governor mopped his forehead with a white handkerchief. 'Fifty gold sovereigns! Not silver pagodas, mind – *gold sovereigns!* A king's ransom!'

Sam, who'd never seen a gold coin in his life, shook his head.

'We simply don't have that kind of money!' The governor tapped his fingers impatiently on the blotter. 'I wrote to the Anthropological Society, asked them to take up a collection and what d'you think they said? *No!*' The governor beckoned him closer. 'Those academicals refused to help. Know why, boy?'

Sam shook his head.

'Your Professor Bogusz has a nasty habit of getting into scrapes! Stole a Tjurunga from the Arrernte and got chased into the desert in Australis – nearly died of sunstroke. Smuggled out a totem of the Haisla in New France and almost got scalped. There's even talk –' he lowered his voice to a hoarse whisper – 'of grave robbing in New Castile! What do you think of that, eh?'

Sam was not in the least surprised. He wondered whether to tell the governor that the Collector had tried to steal Uncle Onay but Lola came back, followed by Bela, carrying a tray.

'Thank you, Bela dear. Fruitcake too, my goodness.'

'A word about Sam, Your Excellency,' Bela said. 'The princess has arranged for him to stay at the bungalow with Lola and her grandfather, for now.

We want the professor back safe of course, but if there's no word...' Bela made a face.

'Might as well send you home, eh, Sammy?' the governor bellowed.

'Her manservant's left money for Sam's ticket home and paid for the bungalow until the end of the month.'

'Decent of her. Not like most dignitaries, eating a chap out of house and home! I'll take a drop of whisky in my tea, please, Bela.'

'Of course, Your Excellency. I'll see the children out. That servant chap is waiting for them at the gate.'

'We can see ourselves out, Bela,' Lola assured her.

She led Sam towards the main door. 'Let's take a stroll around the grounds and talk to old Mayo,' she whispered.

Dusk had fallen and the white marble statue of the colonel mounted on his horse stood starkly in the evening light.

Sam stopped to stare up at his frozen face, its angry expression matching the portrait perfectly. 'Does he come out this early? It was much later when I saw him before.'

'He'll come if I summon him.' Lola pointed to a stone bench halfway up the drive. 'There. That's where he usually appears. Let's sit down.'

Sam recognised the shapes of the surrounding rhododendron bushes. A prickle of anticipation ran over his skin, as he realised this was exactly where he'd seen the ghost last time. The moon was rising, an ivory sphere in the darkening sky. He looked back at the warm-lit windows of the Residence. He wasn't overly keen to see the ghost again.

'Now, I'll call him,' Lola told Sam.

'How do you do that?' he whispered. 'Do you have to chant, like the other day when we took the case of skulls?'

'With Mayo it's easier, because his spirit is trapped in the statue. I usually close my eyes and picture his ghost. You've seen him, haven't you? Why don't you try it too? It might help.'

Sam closed his eyes and concentrated. The stone bench was cool against his legs. An evening breeze rustled the shiny leaves and cicadas rasped from the trees. He remembered the ghost's white, half-transparent form and shivered.

The whooping call of an owl startled him and he opened his eyes. Lola sat beside him, eyes closed, her foot tapping.

'Should I do that too? Tap my foot?' he asked.

Lola frowned. 'No need. But could you hold on to me? Just in case I go a bit funny.'

Sam reached for her hand – it felt natural to take it in his – when he heard it. The slow clip-clop of hooves.

Opening his eyes, he found himself staring up in terror at the tall white figure on his horse, hands twitching at the reins. It was exactly the size and shape of the marble statue – only it *moved*.

'*What do you want from me?*' The horseman's voice was cracked, but his words were clear. Sam almost fell off the bench. Just as last time, his grating voice seemed to come from every direction at once. The ghost horse towered above them, its great hooves pawing at the ground.

Sam stared at Lola in confusion. Her lips were moving as if she was in conversation with the ghost, although he heard only muddled whispers.

'*Humph,*' the colonel said, frowning. '*All right. You know, I once visited the interior where your people live, to meet your forefathers.*'

Lola's hand grew slack and Sam clutched it tighter in alarm. Her eyes were open and she stared ahead, mumbling like a sleepwalker.

'*Bucephalus will enjoy a proper gallop. Tomorrow, then, at midnight.*' The huge horse shook its mane, whinnied and stamped at the sound of its name. Colonel Mayo glared at Sam. '*Don't stare! Close your mouth, boy.*'

Sam duly shut his mouth. Horse and rider turned, clattering back down the drive towards the Residence and Lola keeled over sideways on top of him.

'Lola. *Lola!*' He shook her awake.

'Be careful,' Lola murmured. 'Uncle Onay said—'

'Come on, Lola – let's get you home.' He helped her stand, rubbing her hands which were icy. 'What did Uncle Onay say?'

'He said,' Lola yawned sleepily, but allowed herself to be led along, 'Onay talked to Mayo. He met him long ago. Uncle Onay said to be careful…'

Sam felt her shiver as he took her arm. She was freezing, as if the ghost's chill had sucked away the evening's balmy warmth. He was relieved to see Sparrow waiting for them in the car.

'Careful of *what?*' he asked. But Lola didn't answer.

Twenty-four

Sam did not sleep well that night. *What if, what if, what if?* The words resounded in his mind, a steady thudding like a heartbeat. What if Sparrow and Ophelia were seen diving from the *Yellow Pearl*? What if the colonel's ghostly gallop didn't distract the guards? What if they fired at the parrots calling *freedom*? What if Jay didn't hear the *Dugong* signal at midnight? What did a dugong sound like, anyway? And why had Uncle Onay told Lola to be careful?

If anything happened to her... Sam forced himself to stop. He needed to rest. Lola was snoring peacefully in the bunk above, apparently untroubled. He must have fallen asleep eventually because Lola shook him awake.

'Come on – let's get breakfast! I'm starving.'

Luckily Sparrow cooked that morning, not Ophelia, and they feasted on eggs tossed with chillies and tomatoes, parathas and mango juice.

'The governor's driver will meet us at the dock. He'll bring the car back to load up the case of skulls, and drive you down to the sea wall tonight,' Sparrow told them.

'Won't he wonder what's going on?' Sam asked.

She shook her head. 'He's been paid enough not to ask questions. It's Jay I'm worried about. Suppose he gets stuck, or finds the tunnel caved in?'

Sam frowned. Those were two *what-ifs* he hadn't thought of. 'If Moon dug that tunnel, it'll be safe,' he reassured her. 'Moon's five years older than me – if he can crawl through, I'm sure your friend can.'

'Especially now he's skinny as a stick of bamboo,' Sparrow sighed. 'I wish you were coming to see us off. But I think Tuke's keen to get on with his raft building.' They turned to look at Tuke, hammering on the verandah.

Lola and Sam hugged Sparrow and Ophelia goodbye.

'You two be careful tonight,' Ophelia warned. 'It's our fault you're caught up in this escapade.'

'And, Sam Singh – come and visit Moonlally the moment you set foot on the mainland,' Sparrow told him. 'I've left money with Bela, as well as your ticket.'

'I will,' Sam nodded, though he wasn't sure when. Before he left the Isle, he had to solve the mystery of Moon's disappearance. He wasn't going home until he found his brother. He would ask at the port, and if that didn't lead anywhere, he'd head north, pirates or no pirates. Moon couldn't have vanished! He had to be *somewhere*.

The day passed quickly. Sam sat in the warm sun helping Tuke and Lola to bind the huge bamboo canes with rope. He was surprised at how sturdy the raft seemed.

'Strong enough to carry two grown men!' Tuke told him, through Lola. 'In the forest we use vines, but ropes are easier.'

They finished work as the vast red sun sank lower, turning the distant sea crimson. Sam rubbed his neck, where he felt an unpleasant prickle of anticipation. His stomach was a tangle of knots; he had no appetite for the simple meal of fruit, bread and cheese that Sparrow had left them. At supper, Tuke and Lola remained in conversation and Sam let their unfamiliar language drift over him. The only word he caught was *dugong*.

He sat, unravelling a frayed end of rope and tried to remind himself he'd felt this way before – every time Moon went out on a job, he'd lie awake until the early hours, waiting for him to return. And when morning came, his brother would be snoring, right beside him. Moon was stealthy as a wildcat and his footsteps never woke Sam.

So why did he feel taut as a strung bow now? He hadn't been this way on the *Yellow Pearl* despite the seasickness. Nor trekking into the forest – not even when the saltie attacked their canoe.

His worst fears overcame him when someone he cared for was in danger. He was scared for Lola. And Sparrow, Ophelia and Tuke – even Jay – although Sam had only met him once. He sighed. The longer you lived, the more people you came to care for and feel afraid for. It was too much. He wondered if his mother felt this way, raising her boys alone for all those years. Perhaps that was why her words to him could be as sharp as a knife blade.

Lola prodded him. 'Come on, Sam, stop fretting. The moon's rising. We need to get these people to the water, so their spirits can be set free.'

With all his worrying, the evening had passed quickly and night had fallen. The raft was made ready and they helped Tuke pack the skulls carefully back in the case. It was time for their final journey home. Tuke wore a newly woven headdress of palm leaves and Lola had painted his face with clay markings, so he looked regal as the chief he was.

The driver hooted his horn. He helped them load the car and truss the raft on to its roof. Sam saw from the clock on the bungalow wall that it was after eleven.

He whistled for Suka, who plummeted down to land on his shoulder. 'Suka! It's almost time. Will you tell your friends to fly to the Octopus, that big black building on the sea front? But don't cry "freedom" until Tuke tells you.'

'*Freedom!*' agreed Suka. '*Tuke!*'

'Good boy!' Sam told him as Suka glided over to join the flock. He hoped the guards at the prison wouldn't fire their guns at him. He couldn't bear to think of his friend getting hurt.

The car set off down the hillside, the yellow beams of its headlights illuminating the winding turns ahead. Geckos scuttled away into the overgrown roadside and an owl whooped above. Tuke sat silently in front with the driver, his window wound down, Sam and Lola at the back. Suka and the other parrots wheeled silently over the car, their green feathers silvered by moonlight, like a company of spirits already set free.

They trundled closer to the port. The floodlight of the Octopus swept slowly over the landscape, its white beam turning towards them and dazzling the driver, who pulled his visor down against its glare. Tuke shielded his eyes and turned to mutter crossly to Lola.

'Tuke hates electric lights,' she told Sam. 'None of our people like them. In the forest, after sunset, there's only the moon and stars, fireflies and the cooking fire. This blinding brightness feels wrong to us at night.'

The driver pulled over by the sea wall, where a flight of steps with an iron handrail led steeply down to the endless expanse of shifting water. Sam got out, lugging the case of skulls down the steps with the driver. There was a small platform at the bottom where he and Lola would launch the raft, which had a rope attached to one end.

Sam scanned the water's surface for any sign of the *Dugong*. The bay was still, the rippling sea lit by a giant moon, gold as butter. He leaned over the railing to look along the sea wall, searching for the tunnel entrance. But in the darkness, it was impossible. The weathered black stone was draped in long clumps of green seaweed. Waves crashed against the bluffs either side of them; he could taste the salty sea spray.

Tuke called down. They hurried to help him carry the bamboo raft and set it on the platform on top of two cylindrical canes to act as slides. Sam helped Lola lift the skulls delicately from the case on to the raft, marigold petals still clinging to them. When they were done, he stepped back to survey their work. The skulls were neatly arrayed, their bony vaults taking on a soft glow in the full moon. As the clouds shifted, moonlight reflected from eye sockets, glinting as if the spirits within were stirring awake.

'Sam Singh!' Lola nudged him out of his reverie. 'Wake up! I need you to hang on to this rope. Once we've released the raft, we run up the steps. The tide rises quickly here.'

Sam looped the rope attached to the raft twice round his wrist and gripped it firmly. Tuke nodded, then walked back up the steps. Sam heard the car engine start. The Octopus's lit windows glared at them like giant, watchful eyes.

Up on the sea wall, Tuke rattled his drum and began chanting loudly.

'What's Tuke saying?' he asked Lola.

'He's telling the spirits they're free to ride on the wind to their own lands.' Lola's voice trembled. 'Let go of the rope now, Sam.'

The dazzling beam of the Octopus swung across. A fine mist was rising, thickening to a dense white; behind it, a vague shape loomed. Sam unwound the rope, which was already tugging hard at his wrist and played it out. The bamboo raft was lifted upon the swell. They watched it float, carried out to sea with its strange cargo.

And then the cry came: a high chorus of loud chirping squeaks that filled his ears. The *Dugong* had surfaced.

Twenty-five

Tuke's deep voice sang out, the clatter of his drum reverberating in the air.

'That must be it – their submersible!' Sam pointed to a curved outline taking shape behind the mist.

The water had risen; waves washed over the stairway. Sam took a few steps up, the sea lapping at his ankles.

Lola leaned over the railing below. 'Like the cry the creature makes, only much louder. A hundred dugongs.' Her voice was shaky and Sam saw she was shivering, her body racked by violent shudders, like when he was seasick on the *Yellow Pearl.*

'Lola! We should go up and wait with Tuke.'

'What's that?' Lola hung further over the railing, gazing along the sea wall. Sam peered into the gloom – he could make out a figure in a black rubber suit clinging to the wall. Was it Sparrow? The figure fastened a wire to an iron hoop and tugged. The wire shot taut and Sam saw that a harness was attached to it, so they could abseil back to the *Dugong*.

Cool water lapped at his knees. With each incoming wave, the water was surging rapidly higher. 'Lola – come on!' he called, as he waded up the steps. 'Start climbing!' A tell-tale clatter of hooves rang out over the crash of breakers and then came the squawks of *freedom* from the parrots. 'Colonel Mayo!' he exclaimed. 'It worked, Lola!'

Just as he reached the top, Tuke's chant broke its rhythm with a shout of fear. Sam turned back to see a huge wave break upon the steps, sweeping high above Lola, and flinging her, helpless as a doll, over the rail into the sea.

'*Lola!*' he screamed. 'Tuke, help—'

But Tuke was still chanting, his drumbeat unbroken. Hadn't he seen her fall in? Sam scanned the dark waters frantically for movement. He waded back down the flooded steps, clinging to the handrail, seawater now rushing above his waist. The mist had thinned but there was no sign of her.

'Lola!' he shouted again. '*Lola!*'

'*Sam Singh!*' Suka swooped down to perch beside him.

'Suka – fly across the water and find Lola! She's been taken by the sea!' he cried.

'*Lola!*' Suka squawked. '*Find Lola!*' and he took off.

Sam looked desperately for Lola's bobbing head. She was a good swimmer so where *was* she? He heard Tuke's chants ringing from the sea wall and his drum rattling over the wind, until an ear-splitting alarm blared from the prison, drowning out all other sounds.

There was nothing else for it. Sam took a deep breath and dived in.

The saltwater embraced him, shockingly cold. He tried to remember what Moon had taught him when he first learned to swim in the river, his mother washing clothes nearby. *Don't thrash your arms. If you're tired, turn on your back and float. Stay calm. Let the water carry you.*

Sam surfaced, coughing and spluttering. He trod water, wondering what to do when he spotted a dark line against the moon's silver wake, bobbing a distance away. It was the bamboo raft! If he could only reach it and climb on, he could search for Lola. There was no chance of saving her if he let himself drown.

He swam steadily, trying not to swallow too much briny water, or panic at how far he'd come from shore. He could no longer hear Tuke's voice, and the closer he swam to the raft, the further it drifted. At last, when he'd almost given up, something brushed his shoulder – the rope! He pulled it towards him, paddling with one hand, then grabbed the raft edge and flopped himself on, gasping until his breath steadied.

The floodlight from the Octopus spun round, its brilliant glare lighting the water. Sam sat up, shielding his eyes and searching the surface.

'*Lola!*' he shouted again, his voice dying in the wind. He turned back to the Octopus as the light swung slowly inland. Tuke would have gone for help, surely? But for now, Sam was alone.

Almost. While most of the skulls had been washed overboard, one was lodged in the centre of the raft. The dark hollows of its eyes were empty. Sam did not mind its company now the spirit had been released, but he knew he had to complete the ritual and give it a final resting place on the seabed below.

His own people buried their dead in a forest clearing, far from any villages or settlements, with a handful of rice scattered over them and a coin in each hand. He didn't have any rice or coins, but he knew the words you recited for the dead. He'd had to say them for his own father when he was tiny.

A few bedraggled flowers clung between the bamboo shafts. He pulled away their petals, and chanted, 'Here is your resting place. Come back no more, take your spirit elsewhere and do not trouble us,' while scattering them on the water. Then, he gently lifted the skull and lowered it overboard, to be swallowed by the waves. The mist hovering over the sea seemed to eddy and swirl, and the water seethed.

Sam felt a shiver run down his spine. He knew it was to do with the spirits, drifting over the sea.

The raft tipped with the swell and Sam shuffled back to the centre. Remembering the rope, he lashed it around his waist, knotting it tight, in case a big wave washed over and took him with it. He stared up at the stars, making a glittering white river across the night sky. Until Suka returned, he was stranded on a bamboo raft, drifting towards open sea.

Twenty-six

Sam woke with a start, licking salt from his cracked lips and blinking his stinging eyes. He wasn't sure how long he'd been on the water – an hour, maybe two, or three. It was still night. The black sky had clouded over to hide the full moon. But the bamboo raft, soundly built by Tuke, remained afloat.

Around him, the sea stirred. He heard a chorus of cheeps, above a deeper rumbling and recognised the sound of the *Dugong*. Fainter than on the shore – but the craft had to be out there somewhere!

'Help! I'm here!' he tried to shout, his voice hoarse from the salty air.

Nothing. The chirping filled his ears, louder this time, surrounding him. Then a round grey head poked out of the water. The creature had a snout and a friendly face, as if smiling, and was followed by another, then another. Wherever one appeared, the sea shimmered with a ghostly light. Sam stared.

Dugongs. Real dugongs, a whole herd! The animals ducked and resurfaced, regarding him curiously, as if they were trying to tell him something. And what was that strange light on the sea? Sam trailed his hand in the water, marvelling at the luminous blue glow, gleaming wherever he disturbed it.

More of the herd were barrelling towards him; one was carrying something. Sam rubbed his eyes in disbelief. It was Lola – he recognised her hair and red dress – draped over the back of a large dugong.

'Lola!' he shouted. '*Lola!* Over here!'

The creature made a grunting cry, as if it had heard him. It *had* heard him, or seen him, Sam realised, because it was coming closer.

'Bring her here!' he shouted. '*Lola!*'

The dugong swam up beside the raft, clumsily nudging it sideways. Sam struggled to his knees and reached to grab Lola's shoulders, pulling her towards him. She was unconscious, her arms floppy, but he managed to drag her on to the raft which wobbled dangerously but stayed afloat.

'Thank you – *thank you!*'

The large dugong grunted, as if it was saying, *no bother*, then sank slowly into the sea. The rest of the herd, their heads poking out of the water, echoed with a cacophony of grunts and cheeps. And then they were gone, diving under to follow their leader.

'Lola! *Lola!*' Sam tried feeling for her pulse, as he'd seen Ophelia do, but her wrists were too cold. Her eyes wouldn't open but when he held his hand to her mouth, he felt a warm breath. Lola was alive. Drops of seawater glimmered in her hair and her lips were tinged blue but she looked peaceful, as if she were only sleeping.

What should he do now? Out on a bamboo raft, far from shore and with no paddle? Sam tried not to panic, though his mouth felt puckered and his throat parched. They were in trouble without fresh water. Why hadn't Suka come back?

He tried to remember what he knew about dugongs. When he'd asked Lola about whales, she'd told him that the sea mammals lived in the mangrove swamps and didn't venture far from shore. Did that mean he was close to land? He couldn't tell in the dark, but if the bamboo raft stayed afloat until first light, he might see the shoreline.

They drifted on, until at last, the sky's enveloping black became deepest blue. On the horizon, a fiery orange line meant sunrise was near. Dizzy with thirst, Sam felt hope hammer in his chest. His eyes blurred as he searched for the outline of the Isle. Finally, there it was – a dark silhouette, like the curved back of a great turtle, its lush green interior still far away.

How would he steer the raft without so much as a paddle? He had to find help soon – he *had* to! Then he heard a sound so welcome, his dry eyes ached.

'*Sam Singh! Lola!*'

'Suka! Where have you *been*? I found Lola. But we need help – quick. Lola's sick.'

Suka landed on the raft with a fluttering of wings and regarded Lola, head to one side.

'*Lola sick!*' he agreed. '*Malade, beemar!*'

'We need help, Suka. Fresh water – or we'll die!'

'*Help! Au secours!*' the parrot crowed and took off again towards the open sea. '*Help Sam! Help Lola!*'

'Suka, wait – where are you going? The Isle's back that way!'

Surely Suka wouldn't abandon him again?

He looked down at Lola. She'd stirred once or twice but hadn't opened her eyes. What if no one found them? They might drift on and on for ever. Desperately, Sam searched the skies until he saw

Suka darting swiftly towards them. The parrot hovered over the raft, flapping his wings and crying, '*Help Sam Singh! Help Lola!*'

And then the most beautiful sight ever. Sam saw the submarine's sleek curve emerge from the waves like a whale – or a mighty dugong. The glass rooflight slid open and the small figure in a diving suit slipped into the water. A minute later they were clutching the edge of the raft.

'Rope, Sam! Throw me the *rope.*'

It was Sparrow's muffled voice – he saw her face through the window of her helmet. Sam could have kissed her. Quickly, he untied the rope from around his waist and passed it to her. Sparrow swam, tugging the raft and Sam paddled with his hands to help.

Close up, the *Dugong* was huge. A curved ovoid, like a gigantic fish. In the pale dawn light, the skin of the vessel gleamed, its metallic tiles overlapping like scales. As well as the glass roof, there was a round amber window, a giant eye. Someone was in there, pulling levers and peering at dials.

A hatch swung open, and a ladder dropped. Ophelia and Jay, still in his black prison garb, helped Sparrow scramble inside. Then he climbed down, slung Lola over his shoulder and beckoned Sam to follow.

Sam clambered up, legs collapsing under him, and rolled into the *Dugong* as the bamboo raft bobbed away. The hatch swung shut as the sun broke over the horizon, blinding him with its light. He lay on his back, too exhausted to move, his stomach lurching as the submersible sank beneath the waves. Through the glass rooflight above, he watched the amber sky become sea; the cabin around him bathed with watery green light. A shoal of black-striped grouper drifted overhead.

Inside the cabin, small lamps flickered. By their warm glow, he saw Jay carry Lola to a camp bed and Ophelia kneel to check her pulse. Bright spots swam before his eyes and his head ached.

'Water!' he heard Sparrow's voice say. 'He's dehydrated. Lola too!'

'I'll check her gag reflex,' he heard Ophelia say, then Sparrow was crouching in front of him with a bottle, her hair a tangled knot. She held it to his lips and he drank gratefully – the same lemon-flavoured concoction she'd given him on board the *Yellow Pearl*.

'Thank you,' he remembered to say this time. 'Thank you for saving us.'

Twenty-seven

Everything around him blurred for a while. Sam was cold all over and beginning to shiver. Sparrow wrapped him in a blanket and he must have fallen asleep, for when he blinked awake, he was warm and lying on a cosy pile of cushions beside a low table. Lola lay on a bunk further down the cabin, Ophelia watching her.

Sam looked up through the rooflight at the turquoise water. A school of silvery rays flapped elegantly over the glass. He sat up, excitement thrilling him into alertness. He was actually inside the *Dugong*, travelling beneath the sea!

Sparrow and Jay were gazing at a map by soft orange lamplight, talking in low voices.

'Sam's awake!' Sparrow noticed. 'Can you manage a drink? Important to rehydrate.'

She offered him a cup and he drank thirstily. Sam realised, as he tasted the tea's medicinal tang, he didn't feel seasick at all. In fact, he was starving. His stomach gave a thunderous rumble.

'Would you like a biscuit, Sam? I'm afraid we're not kitted out for cooking in here.'

The biscuit was sweet, spiced with cinnamon and the most delicious thing he had ever eaten. Even in lean times with the tribe, he couldn't remember being this hungry. The other two were looking at him expectantly.

'We'd love to hear what happened – when you're ready.' Sparrow smiled.

Sam nodded. 'Lola?' he croaked. 'Is she awake?'

'She's coming round!' Ophelia called. 'Nasty gash on her head, but no sign of internal bleeding.'

What did all those words mean? 'Is she... all right?' he managed.

'Right as rain,' Sparrow reassured him. 'You sound like a frog – you must have swallowed a load of seawater.'

'What about Moon?' Sam turned to Sparrow's friend. 'Can you tell me anything?'

Jay, his dark eyes huge in his thin face, gave him a strained smile, the smile of someone who was out of practice. 'Moon's your brother?'

'That's right!' Sparrow topped up Sam's tea and pushed another biscuit into his hand. 'Please tell Sam what you know, Jay – anything at all.'

Jay shook his head. 'I'm sorry, I don't know much. I learned about the tunnel from the other prisoners – only rumours, but it was worth a shot. I paid off the guards to move into that cell – cell 420. I found the tunnel bricked up, but it wasn't hard to dismantle. When I peered inside, I saw the words *Moon was here* scratched into the roof.'

'That explains the bad poetry,' Sparrow laughed, reciting:

Condemned alone to this cell.
I have a friend though none can tell.
His silver beams do light my way,
From lonely night to bright new day.

Jay winced. 'I wish you wouldn't go on about my poetry – I thought it was clever! Anyway, I explored the tunnel – it led to an old sewage pipe – one they'd stopped using because it flooded. And the pipe led to the sea wall.'

'Moon *must* have escaped the same way,' Sparrow put in.

Jay nodded. 'Very likely.' He rubbed his eyes. 'I can't believe I'm here, talking to you right now.

Everything happened so fast, like a dream. I heard the *Dugong*'s signal. Then a sea fog came down thick. I was still unbricking the opening, but I could barely see my hand in front of my face! And as I started crawling down the tunnel, I heard a mad commotion from the jail – voices crying freedom, galloping horses, guards running along the roof. What was all that about?'

'You wouldn't believe us if we told you!' Sparrow said, winking at Sam. 'We know Moon and the others escaped to the sea wall, and there was a boat waiting to take them away.'

Sam tightened his grip on the cup. 'The superintendent said their boat sank. But I don't believe Moon's gone. Lola's grandfather told me his spirit wasn't in the realm of the dead.'

'I'm sure you're right,' Sparrow said kindly. 'Perhaps they were rescued?'

Sam knew Moon hadn't drowned at sea. His brother was alive. But *where*?

'Why didn't he come home—' His voice cracked. He'd missed his brother badly these last three years. Things might have been different if Moon was home to stick up for him.

'Home to *Indica*?' Jay frowned. 'Your brother would be a wanted man on the mainland – soon caught and sent back here.'

Sam met Jay's tired gaze. 'Does that mean you can't go home either?' he asked.

There was no mistaking the sadness in Jay's tone. 'Not unless there's an amnesty for political prisoners. And that's a way off… if it ever comes. I'm heading east – far from Indica.'

Sparrow sighed 'Let's not talk about that now, Jay. Sam, what about you and Lola? How did you end up on a raft in the middle of the sea? If it hadn't been for Suka—'

'Hang on, where *is* Suka?'

'He's flying above, don't worry. You can whistle for him when we breach. Tell us what happened.'

Sam told them. About the gathering mist, eerily lit by the white floodlight, while the bamboo raft bearing the skulls of the dead was tugged out to sea.

'This huge wave – it came out of nowhere – dragged Lola over the rail and into the water.'

He paused as his raspy voice gave, taking a gulp of tea to soothe his throat and went on in a whisper, 'It's to do with the people. The *skulls.* Lola fainted before when she spoke to them. She can talk with spirits, like her grandfather,' he explained to Jay.

'Then what did you do?' Sparrow asked.

'I – I jumped in after her. I didn't know *what* to do. I could hear Tuke chanting, but I wasn't sure he'd seen! I grabbed hold of the bamboo raft – the one with the skulls – and climbed on to look for Lola. She's a good swimmer – better than me. I didn't know I'd get swept so far out.'

'Sam Singh, you're a hero – you jumped in to save your friend!' Sparrow cried.

Sam shrugged. 'Anyone would have done the same. Then – I must have fallen asleep, because—' He knew the next part of his story would sound strange: the shimmering blue water, the friendly dugongs lifting their heads to greet him. And Lola, like a mermaid, her hair sparkling with droplets of light.

Jay and Sparrow were sitting forward eagerly.

'When I woke up, there was this strange light on the waves. It glowed bright blue.'

'Phosphorescence,' Sparrow explained. 'It's made by tiny creatures in the water. Go on, Sam!'

'I heard grunts and chirps – at first, I thought it was the signal from this submersible. But they were real dugongs! They surrounded the raft and I saw the largest one carrying Lola, draped over its back. It swam beside me and I managed to drag her on to the raft. I know it sounds unbelievable, but it's true.'

'Of course, it's true, Sam Singh! Tuke sent the dugong herd to rescue me. He knew I was in trouble.' The sleepy voice came from the bunk. Lola was awake.

Twenty-eight

There was an outcry and a sudden bustle of activity around Lola's bunk.

'She's awake! Don't move, Lola – I need to check you over.' Ophelia opened a small case of instruments.

'I'm *fine*.' Lola tried to climb off the bed. 'I don't need to be checked. And you're not putting a needle in my arm! Don't you see? I wasn't *sick*, I was in too deep, that's all! Uncle Onay warned me to be careful.'

Lola meant that she had entered the spirit realm too deeply. Sam tried to say so, but no one heard.

'Lie down, Lola – you might have a head injury! Please keep still. You've had a miraculous escape,' Ophelia fussed.

'I don't *want* to lie down,' Lola protested. 'And there's nothing miraculous about it – Tuke sent the dugongs for me!'

Sam looked up as an unfamiliar figure opened a door at the end of the cabin – an older man with a shiny metallic right hand.

'What's all this noise about? Sounds like a riot!'

'Sorry, sir. Miss Ophelia's trying to doctor Lola, and she doesn't want to be doctored.'

The man laughed. 'Can't blame her. Better get back to my post.' He beckoned to Sam. 'Want to see inside, lad? Learn about the *Dugong*'s controls?'

Sam nodded quickly, happy to escape. He shuffled past Lola, still yelling and fighting, and followed the man through the door into the cockpit. Round windows of amber glass bulged on either side, like two great fish eyes. Before him was a dazzling array of wheels, dials, buttons and levers.

'You can go back when its quiet,' the old man said. 'I'm Shri, the captain, I expect the princess mentioned me. What do you think of the *Dugong*?'

'It's amazing!' Sam told him. 'I have a few questions…'

'Ask anything you like. I invented her, you know!'

'What are the silver tiles made of?' Sam began. 'How does it – *she* – move up and down? Why don't other sea creatures attack her?'

'Steady, one question at a time! The outer hull is clad in an aluminium bronze alloy. We run on a system of compressed air. The *Dugong*'s pipes suck in fresh air when we breach – much like a real dugong – and the stale air's compressed and expelled to drive us forward. There are ballast tanks of water, to make the submersible move up and down in the sea.'

Shri went on explaining the workings of the *Dugong,* as the scuffles and shouts from the cabin died away. Lola must have submitted to Ophelia's tests after all. Sam was happily learning about rudders when someone knocked at the cockpit door.

'Lola's asking for you,' Ophelia told him. 'She seems… fully recovered.'

Sam turned to Shri. 'Thank you, sir. May I come back and learn about rudders later?'

'You're welcome any time – bring your friend too!'

Lola was sitting up, with a thin glass tube sticking out of her mouth. '*Mm-mm!*' was all she could say, her hands waving wildly.

'One more minute with that thermometer and then you can talk!' Ophelia warned. 'Whatever you do, don't bite!'

But Sam understood. She was trying to say his name, Sam *Singh*! The way she always did. A grin broke over his face.

Sparrow made more tea for everyone, then it was time for the *Dugong* to breach. Sam sat next to Lola on the narrow bunk as the ship floated slowly towards sunlight. He gave a deep sigh of happiness. A new day had broken, and Lola was better – if quieter than usual. She sat staring into her tea, blowing to cool it.

Sam nudged her. 'What's the matter?'

Lola sighed. 'Sam, I need to get home. I was in the spirit realm for a long time last night.' She hesitated. 'They told me so much – it was hard to understand. I must return to the village and talk to Tuke.'

'What do you mean? Who's *they*?'

'The *spirits*! They're from different tribes, all over the world, and...' Lola's voice tailed off. 'Never mind. I just need to go home.'

'You can tell me, Lola.'

Lola shook her head. 'I've talked to Princess Sparrow. She's agreed to turn the *Dugong* around and head back to the Isle. They're going to leave me on shore, near our dry season camp. I'll make my way from there. Tuke will be home by now. It's time I learned all that he can teach me – before it's too late.'

'What can I do?' Sam asked. 'I want to come back to the village with you.'

Lola shook her head firmly. 'You're a good friend, Sam, but we need to do this for ourselves.'

Sam was silent for a moment. 'If you go now, we won't see each other again.'

Lola looked away. For a moment, Sam was sure there were tears in her eyes. 'I suppose this means goodbye,' she said. 'I'll miss *Suka*, of course.'

Sam grinned. Lola was his friend. He couldn't bear the thought of not seeing her and he knew she felt the same, but she wouldn't admit that.

'There's Suka now!' He pointed up through the glass rooflight to a flash of green feathers, looping the skies above.

Twenty-nine

The *Dugong* breached and the glass whirred slowly open. Sea air whirled briskly around the cabin and Suka dived down to land on Sam's knee.

'*Sam Singh! Lola!*' he screeched.

'Ouch! Gently, Suka! Thank you for saving our lives, boy.' Sam scratched the back of his neck and Lola held out her hand for him to climb on.

'Thank you, Suka,' Lola added. 'I'm going to miss you.'

'*Sam miss Lola! Lola miss Sam!*' the parrot replied.

'I suppose I'll miss Sam too.' Lola darted him a glance. 'Come on, Sam – aren't you going to show me round the underwater beast before I go home?'

'Let's ask Shri – he's captain.'

Shri was pleased to see Lola recovered, and delighted to meet Suka, who perched on his metal hand.

'I lost my real hand years ago – this one serves me well. Suka's claws won't hurt, however tight he grips!' Shri demonstrated the controls and left Jay to steer while he showed them the rest of the ship.

The *Dugong* was a wonderful craft, with lots packed into its small space: folding bunks for sleeping, comfortable chairs – even a tiny kitchen and bathroom. Sam explained how it worked, with Shri's beaming approval. The old man showed them how to operate the ballast tanks of saltwater, which was released to make the craft rise, and desalinated for drinking.

Schools of rainbow-coloured fish, silver rays and a small shark passed over the rooflight as the *Dugong* wheeled slowly to set its course. The only food on board was dried or tinned, but Sparrow insisted Sam and Lola eat a meal of crackers, tomato chutney and tinned anchovies.

Next time they breached, the Isle was closer. Shri asked them to describe the beach where they were to drop off Lola – the site of the crocodile attack.

'I think I know it. That bay's too shallow for the *Dugong*, so we'll use a lifeboat – we've got a couple tucked away in these cupboards.' He slid open a cabin door to reveal two canoes.

'I can paddle Lola to the beach?' Sparrow called.

'No – I want to take Lola back.' Sam was worried about what had happened to her out on the water. This would be his last chance to ask – and to say goodbye.

'Are you strong enough, Sam? The currents are swift here. Wasn't the Collector swept away?'

Sam felt a touch of guilt at the mention of the Collector, still captive and awaiting a ransom no one would pay. Or had the pirates, as rumoured, begun to cut off his fingers and send him back in pieces? He didn't regret taking the stolen skulls, or helping Tuke and Lola free the spirits inside. But he did feel somehow responsible for the man.

Lola smiled at him. 'I'd like that.' She turned to the others. 'Of course Sam's strong enough – we rowed the dugout from the village. And there's no danger of drifting out to sea because you'll be right here. Also, I won't have to worry about that big saltie, because Sam stabbed it in the eye and—'

'Sam did what?' Jay shook his head.

Sparrow and Jay exchanged glances. 'All right. Row straight to the beach and back.'

'It's time we breached,' Shri called from the cockpit. 'Would you two like to operate the controls?'

They hurried in. Sam pulled the ballast lever and water flooded out of the saltwater tanks that weighted the submersible. As the *Dugong* lifted above the waves, Lola pushed the button that slid the glass rooflight open. They ran out into the cabin and climbed up to peek over the edge.

'*Land ahoy! Kinara dekho!*' screeched Suka, who soared into the sky.

The turtle-shaped Isle grew rapidly closer. Sam saw its shiny black stone cliffs and silvery volcanic sand without the huddled houses of the port or the hulking Octopus. From here, the Isle appeared as it always had done: a green-and-jet jewel sparkling in blue seas. It was so beautiful Sam felt a pang at the thought of leaving it. And Moon? Was he still on the island somewhere, trapped or injured? He remembered how Tuke had found his brother's spirit, alive but dimmed.

Jay's head popped up beside them.

'Looks pretty close!' he warned. 'What's the maximum depth, Shri?'

'Fifteen!' Shri shouted from the cockpit.

'Tide's due to turn – let's launch now!'

The *Dugong*'s lifeboat slid sleekly along tracks to the hatch and Sam climbed into the lightweight craft, so different from the heavy dugout canoes. The paddles were new, wide-tipped and coated in rubber. He slotted them into position, while Lola said her goodbyes.

'Lola – I know you don't need our help. But if you or your people ever do, wire me. I'll do everything I can,' Sparrow told her.

Lola nodded. 'I know,' she said simply. 'Good luck, Jay. And thank you all – for everything. Come on, Sam!'

Sam's arms felt a little shaky, but he soon found a rhythm and the craft sped rapidly towards the beach, Suka flying above.

'We're a good team, Sam Singh,' Lola told him.

'We are,' Sam agreed sadly. 'Lola, please tell me about last night. What did those people say to you – the spirits of the skulls?'

Lola sighed. 'I'm not sure you want to hear this.'

'I do, I promise.'

She shrugged. 'You have saved my life *twice* now. I suppose I should tell you. Stop paddling for a bit.'

Sam pulled the paddles in to rest at the bottom of the boat.

Lola pressed her hands over her eyes. 'It was *horrible*, Sam! I can still see their faces appearing from the mist... they wanted to warn me of what happened after strangers came to their lands.' She shook her head. 'Some said thousands of their people died, just like my parents. Some were massacred by the invaders. Their lands were taken, forests and rivers – all taken, Sam!' Lola's eyes filled with tears.

Sam nodded. He knew how Lola felt. He remembered the greeting of his own tribe of land pirates.

We are kings of the forest.
Let them tame us if they can!

But now the trees were felled, the animals frightened away and his people were left to wander the cities, selling trinkets, stealing stray hens and picking the odd pocket.

'The spirits told me that unless we stop strangers coming into the Isle's interior – we won't survive either! Those who warned me, said all their tribespeople are gone. Whole families, whole tribes, whole worlds died out. Nothing can ever bring them back.'

Sam was silent, as the boat drifted over the shallows.

'Lola – I do understand. But I'll miss you. And I want to know what happens. If I send you a letter at the Governor's Residence, will you reply?'

'Of course! And if I hear anything about Moon, I'll write straight away. Someone must have heard of an escaped prisoner with a scorpion tattoo!'

Sam blinked back his tears. He'd come to the Isle of Lost Voices to look for his brother and though he hadn't found Moon, he had something else – a true friend.

Lola looked around. A gentle tide had carried the lifeboat effortlessly towards the beach. She smiled. 'I'll walk from here. You watch for salties, Sam.'

Sam nodded miserably. 'I can come up to the cliff with you – just in case?'

Lola shook her head. 'Easier if you don't. Promise to write, Sam Singh – and I promise, I'll find your brother.'

'*Goodbye, Lola! Goodbye, Sam Singh!*' Suka spiralled up into the blue sky overhead.

'Suka – every time I hear a parrot squawking, I'll remember you!' Lola called. She jumped out and Sam watched her splash through the shallows. He scanned the beach carefully, but Lola was hopping up the steps carved into the cliff. She turned at the top, waved, and was gone.

'*Danger!*' Suka screeched suddenly, plunging in a zig-zag path over the water. '*Danger! Khatra!*'

'What's up, Suka? What danger?' Sam swept his gaze over the turquoise water and gently foaming waves.

In the distance, the *Dugong*'s silver curve sank beneath the sea. Sam knew it was waiting to take him home. He looked up at the empty clifftop and took up his paddles. They felt heavier, as if weighed down by what he was leaving behind: a brother and his best friend.

The stern of the boat had spun round, almost lodging in the sand. Sam braced his shoulders and began to row backwards, his eyes on the cliffs. He thought of Lola making her way to the village, and how relieved Tuke would be to see her. The villagers would hold a huge feast – someone would kill a pig – and she'd sit by the fire at twilight – firefly time – to tell them of her adventures.

He looked up at the sky and whistled for Suka, but the parrot had flown away. The canoe was drifting off course. Using his paddle, he worked it around in the water so he was facing forward – but something tugged at the bow, swinging the boat so it pointed towards the shore again.

What was going on? Was he caught in a riptide? He lifted the paddles to row, when the boat was suddenly dragged swiftly on, without Sam doing a thing. He twisted to see a taut wire snagged over the bow with a grapple hook. He was being towed! Had the *Dugong* decided to pull him in? But he was being carried in the wrong direction.

The canoe was sluicing rapidly through the calm sea. Sam lunged to detach the hook and heard shouts. He looked up to see a wooden schooner moving inescapably closer, its dark beams rotted and sails ragged and torn. Two men on deck grinned and waved. They didn't look friendly. Why were they towing him – did they think he was in trouble?

That was when he saw the red flag fluttering from the ship's mast. An ivory skull-and-crossbones on scarlet cloth; it was the flag of the Isle's chief pirate, the Jalai Rajah.

Thirty

As Sam struggled to free the hook, the ship sidled closer – so alarmingly near he could see the pirates' scowling faces, tattooed chests, and the lethal cutlasses carelessly resting in their hands. There must have been twenty of them – crowding the deck, leaning over the galley, and rowing towards him.

He scrambled to his feet, ready to dive in and swim for his life, when a rope dropped from the sky, lassoing his shoulders and pinning his arms. And then the pirates were on him, blindfolding his eyes, tying his hands behind his back, stuffing a rag in his mouth and bundling him over their shoulder, up the ladder until – *bang!* – he was thrown down, his face smacking hard against the rough, splintered wood of the deck.

Ouch! Sam lay there, momentarily stunned.

As he came to, he began to wriggle his wrists free. He was trussed tight as a chicken, but managed to spit the rag out. Flopping on to his back, he turned his head side to side to work the knotted blindfold loose against the slanting deck. The ship pitched sharply beneath him.

'The Jalai Rajah's going to be pleased as a parrot to see today's haul! Nice little craft for slinking in and out of Deadman's Cave!' someone shouted.

'Aye, a good day's work – to think we only came to finish off that one-eyed saltie!' another added.

One-eyed saltie! Sam gulped, recalling the croc he'd stabbed.

'She'd make a neat fishing vessel!' another returned.

'Fishing vessel? *Fishing* vessel!' a voice jeered. 'Are we *fisherman*, by the Jalai Rajah? What are we, hearties?'

'Pirates and plunderers!' came the shouts.

'And the boy?' another voice asked. 'What shall we do with him?'

Sam shifted his blindfold a little and strained to hear the man's muttered reply.

'He'll be put to work – and if he don't work, the sharks can feast on him. Not going to raise no ransom for that little runt.'

'Not managed a ransom for that professor yet, for all we was promised!' another grumbled.

'Aye. Two gold coins apiece, the Rajah said.'

Sam took a deep breath, his mind racing. *Professor?* The pirates had to be talking about the Collector. He tried not to panic, knowing the *Dugong* was lurking close by. Hopefully it was following the pirate ship. Suka had spotted the pirates and cried danger – if only Sam had listened!

By now, Sam had half-loosened the knotted ropes and with a twist of his arms would be free. He'd shifted the bandana tied over his eyes and could just about see. So far, the pirates hadn't bothered to search him – his knife was safely hidden under his loose shirt in its leather sheath. He wasn't afraid. To these men, he might look like a helpless kid, but he was a land pirate. He just had to wait for the right time to act.

Sam heard splashing oars and cries of, 'Heave to!' as they rowed on. They couldn't have gone more than a kilometre when he heard one of the crew shout the command to drop anchor. Then, to his dismay, two of them held him down as another searched him, quickly finding Moon's knife.

'Nice piece. Too good for a runt like you!' Sam took a cuff to the head, then a hard punch to his stomach that winded him.

'*Ow!*' He curled up in pain, careful to keep his wrists pressed together, hoping they wouldn't see the loosened knots.

He was flung back into the *Dugong*'s lifeboat, which sat low in the water. Two others piled in beside him but the rest of the crew stayed on board. Where were they taking him now? He'd heard something about Deadman's Cave. They had to be on the Isle's coastline; the ship hadn't sailed far enough to touch ground elsewhere.

'Get rowing, boys. Did you hear that racket? What are them sea pigs doing round here? That ain't usual,' one of the men growled over the splash of paddles. Sam listened. There it was! A rapid chorus of dugong chirps. The *Dugong* crew were sending him a signal!

'I hear they taste good as meat if you roast them,' the other replied. 'Let's go harpooning tonight.'

'You'll be blind drunk and too clumsy to harpoon a sea pig tonight or any night,' the first spat. 'Put your back into rowing! Slow down when you come to Finger Rock.'

The boat rolled unsteadily, slamming the rocks with a crunch every now and then, and Sam felt the sting of saltwater dash his face.

'Right, lad. Welcome to our humble abode.'

Sam was dragged out, pulled roughly to his feet and he staggered on to solid ground. He sensed he was in a dark, cool place, sheltered from the burning sun, but could still hear the steady crash and hiss of breaking waves. The pirates had rowed right inside Deadman's Cave.

He felt something hard and cold press into the small of his back, and a grouchy voice said, 'Keep walking. And don't try any funny business.'

He was marched along, prodded by what he guessed was a gun. Hoping to learn more, he pretended to trip and fall sideways and his face scraped against uneven, jagged stone.

'Get up!' the voice echoed eerily around him.

They had to be inside a cave – would the *Dugong* be able to follow?

Sam was pushed on, until by the echo of footsteps and a fresh breeze, he realised they were in a larger space. His heart sank as he heard more footsteps and a low murmur of voices. How many pirates were here? It sounded like a whole village! The *Dugong* had no weapons on board that he'd seen – while the pirates had cutlasses and at least one pistol.

Even if the others did come to his rescue, there was no way they could fight their way out.

He would have to use his wits instead.

Thirty-one

A clamour of angry voices surrounded him.
 'Who brung that runt back in the first place? Should have took the boat and left him in the water,' a gruff voice complained. 'He ain't worth nothing.'

'He can work, can't he? And join us when he's grown,' another replied.

'We got no shortage of men – he's another mouth to feed! Don't know what the Jalai Rajah's going to say to this.'

'Let's ask him.'

'Are you mad? He's already started on the rum.'

'We'll tell him tomorrow. Either the runt stays and works, or we tie him to a rock and drop him in the lagoon.'

'Agreed. Bung him down the hole with the other one for now.'

Sam didn't like the sound of this. He was shoved into a narrow passage which sloped steeply downwards, the gun's muzzle pressed painfully into his back, then jostled into another space, where he stumbled to the rocky floor.

'Don't move from that spot! Or I've got a bullet with your name on!' a voice growled.

Sam waited until the men's footsteps faded to silence, then wriggled free from the ropes and tore off his blindfold, rubbing his tender wrists while his eyes adjusted to the dim light.

He stared around in wonder. The inside of the cave was pale as sun-bleached bone, its walls shirred and pleated in tall columns, curving to a roof high above. Here and there, crops of sharp pinnacles hung down. He scrambled to his feet and reached to touch the rough stone. It felt like he was imprisoned in the skull of a giant animal.

The light came from an oil lantern, burning in a shadowy corner. Sam stared, catching a movement by its yellow glow. What he'd mistaken for a heap of rags was a person. Sam took a step closer. Despite his scruffy appearance, there was no mistaking him.

'Professor Bogusz!'

'Who's there?' The Collector's hands were tied and he struggled upright.

'Sir, it's me, Sam Singh.' Sam frowned. Why couldn't he shake his habit of being polite? The Collector hardly deserved it.

'*Parrot boy?* Did the governor send you with my ransom?'

'No, sir. They captured me in a small boat, just like you.'

'Dash it! I expected the governor to have stumped up the gold by now!'

'Well, he tried, sir. He's written to the Anthro... something?'

'Anthropological Society – I'm a prominent member. Not that these outlaws respect the intellect. Although, their lingo is fascinating – a mix of Laskari, Malay – even a few words of your own land-pirate tongue! They took my notebook, or I'd have transcribed a good amount by now.'

'You can't write with your hands tied behind your back,' Sam pointed out.

'Precisely! What are you waiting for, boy – come and untie me!'

Sam padded quietly over and crouched beside the knotted ropes. 'Keep your voice down – we can't let them know we're free,' he whispered.

But the Collector boomed on. 'They call their leader the Jalai Rajah – the meaning being either *king of the road* or *great king* – a contraction of *Jalili*—'

'Shh!' Sam hissed. 'Listen – help's close by. The Princess of Moonlally has a submersible and – well, there's no time to explain. I don't know how long she'll be – but look – I have a trick for your hands.'

Relieved the Collector was listening for once, he showed him a snake knot, an old trick of Moon's. You looped the rope around your wrists as if you were tied up, but you could free yourself with a quick twist.

'Jolly good. I'll sit and scratch some notes with a bit of chalk – these are limestone caves, you know. They took my pistol, or I'd have shot through the chain.'

To his horror, Sam saw he wore an iron shackle around one ankle, with a long chain attached to a nail, embedded in the cave's stone floor.

Footsteps came echoing down the rocky passageway.

'Quick – back as you were,' he told the Collector, hurrying over to retie his blindfold, loop a snake knot around his wrists and fall to the ground.

'Why did yer go and show the Rajah that knife we took? Got him all riled up!' the pirate complained.

'How was I to know?' the second replied in an injured tone. 'Nice little piece, fancy handle

– thought our chief'd be pleased. Would have been worse if I kept it for meself!'

He bent to deliver a clumsy blow to Sam's head. 'You, lad! The Jalai Rajah wants to know where you got that knife.'

'I'll tell him myself,' Sam replied.

'No disrespect – or it's into the lagoon with you!' the first man hissed, taking a fistful of Sam's hair and wrenching his head back. Through one eye, Sam saw his furious face and the gun, an old-fashioned pistol he hoped wasn't loaded.

'Take me to the Jalai Rajah and I'll tell him,' he repeated. 'I need to give him a message from the governor – about the professor here.'

The man growled and shoved Sam's head painfully down against the rock.

'No need for that – he's only a kid,' the other man objected.

'He's bluffing – don't you see? Old blabbermouth in the corner told him about the ransom!'

'Well, I say we take 'im to the Rajah. He won't like us keeping him waiting – better he takes it out on the kid than us.'

The first man spat.

'Come on – get up! You heard him. Quick march!'

The two men pushed him through the narrow passage into a larger cave, Sam shuffling slowly so they wouldn't know he could see. He strained to hear the chirping signal of the *Dugong* – Sparrow and the others had to be planning a rescue – and when they did, he would be ready.

'Right. Tell the Rajah where you got that knife, runt!'

Sam was herded forward. He squinted over the blindfold to get a look at the pirate chief. He was sitting on a boulder jutting into the lagoon, his back turned. He had on a tattered red jacket, like the governor had worn at the ball, only the gold piping on the sleeves was tarnished black.

'Who d'you get this knife off?' the Jalai Rajah grunted. He held Sam's knife up in the air like a question.

The pirate with the gun kicked at his ankle. '*Go on!* Tell the Rajah!'

Sam stared at the sweep of dark water stretching out into the sunlight. That was how the pirates had steered the canoe inside – the entrance was too narrow for their ship. But how deep was it? He wasn't sure the *Dugong* could manoeuvre this far. He noticed a stirring at the surface – something sleek and black bobbed up then went under, its ripples travelling in a wide circle.

Sam's wrists were loose behind his back. This was his moment! Freeing his hands, he leaped on to the rock, and kicked his knife from the pirate's hand. Slinging the rope under the man's chin, he shoved him off the boulder so the Jalai Rajah was dangling.

'No one move!' he shouted. 'Or your chief dies!'

The half-throttled man made a gurgling sound. Sam released the pressure on his neck. He didn't want to kill him – just get out of there. Glancing down, he found himself staring in amazement at a familiar face.

'All right, Sam?' his brother gasped.

Sam released his hold on the rope in shock. Moon slid down the boulder and into the water of the lagoon with a great splash.

Thirty-two

There was a sudden uproar. Several pirates kneeled by the edge, shouting, as Moon surfaced, his flailing arms splashing wildly, then disappeared back under. Sam used the diversion to kick an old pistol and a few cutlasses into the lagoon.

'Someone fetch the mast! Hold it over the water!' one yelled.

'I thought the Rajah could swim?' Another of the men leaned over, peering in.

''Course he can't swim, fool. 'Tis bad luck for a pirate!' said another.

But Sam knew Moon could swim, and swim well. Why was he taking so long to climb out? His brother came up again, gasping for air, then something – or someone – dragged him back.

When Moon finally emerged, two people in black diving costumes were gripping him by the arms. The smaller of the two had the tip of Sam's knife pressed firmly to his neck.

'*Sparrow!*' Sam had never been more relieved to see anyone. Whatever this mess was, he knew she could sort it out.

'Stand back against that wall and drop your weapons,' Sparrow shouted, her voice muffled beneath the diving helmet. 'Or I'll cut your chief's throat!'

The pirates muttered and grumbled but shuffled towards the far wall of the cave. The taller figure pulled his helmet off – it was Jay.

'Line up, face to the wall, all of you,' he shouted. 'Hands in the air! Sam, pass me that gun.' He nodded to the floor, and Sam recognised the ivory-handled pistol belonging to the Collector.

'Sam! This a friend of yours?' Moon called. 'Tell 'im to stop tickling me jugular. I ain't gonna hurt you, am I, little brother? Knew that was your knife the minute I saw it – figured some thug took it off you.' He grinned at Sam. 'Fooled us with the old snake knot. Taught you well, didn't I?'

Sam nodded. He had found Moon – his own brother – but he was different. Everything was different. Moon's face was scarred and thin and older. And he was chief of a nasty bunch of sea pirates. He wanted to say so much, but all he could manage was, 'You did.'

'*Brother?*' Sparrow looked between Moon and Sam. 'You mean this is him – Moon? *Moon* is the Jalai Rajah?' She released his arm and lowered the knife.

'That I am,' Moon bowed with a flourish. 'And Sam's me own brother – nearly tall as me now!'

Sam met Sparrow's gaze and shrugged. 'I'm sorry,' was all he could manage.

'Don't be sorry – it's not your fault. Here, take your knife, Sam.' She pulled off her helmet, her plait uncoiling down her back. Moon stared.

'A *girl?*' he said disbelievingly.

Sam cuffed him on the shoulder. 'Show some respect, brother,' he told him. 'This is the Princess of Moonlally.'

Sometime later, every weapon had been piled into a heap, except the Collector's pistol, which Jay kept, and Sam's own knife. They'd eaten their fill of the pirates' supplies of dried fish and jackfruit jerky, and all the men but Moon had been sent to pass the night on board their ship.

'Now, then. Reckon it's time for a parley. Can't believe you came all this way looking for me, Sam!' Moon marvelled. They were seated around a small fire, smoke drifting to the cave's mouth to meet the spray and rush of the waves.

'I wasn't sure you were on the Isle – not until I found your message in a bottle, with the scorpion scratched on the glass. Lola's grandfather had it.'

'I used your tunnel to escape from the Octopus, Moon,' Jay said. 'The one out of cell number 420 – it's still got your name carved there.'

'The prison superintendent said you'd drowned,' Sparrow put in. 'But Sam wouldn't give up. He was sure you were on the Isle, somewhere.'

Moon shook his head. 'Took three of us a year to dig that tunnel to the sewage pipe. Worked day and night, in shifts. We crawled out and into the fishing boat, waiting. Boat got caught in a storm. The other two didn't make it, but I washed up on a beach not far from here.' He shook his head.

'And the pirates took you in?' Sparrow asked.

Moon scoffed. 'Not exactly. More like I had to fight every one of those ugly mugs for a place on the crew. Old pirate chief died soon after, and no one challenged me.'

Sam didn't wonder. The pirates were nasty ruffians, twice the size of Moon, but his brother was silver-tongued. Moon could talk his way in or out of anything, and for that reason, Sam knew this parley might easily go on all night.

He tried to follow the conversation but felt impossibly tired. He hadn't slept much the night he drifted out to sea, and only napped on board the *Dugong*.

He swallowed. 'Brother – won't you leave this behind and come home? Things aren't the same without you.'

Moon shook his head. 'Not me, Sam. I'm turned sea pirate and couldn't follow land-pirate ways again. Sea roads are faster – not to mention, the takings are better.' His brother gave him a wink and added, 'Besides, from what Jay tells me, I can't go home. I'm a wanted man on the mainland. No one's sending me back to jail.'

Sam nodded. He understood. Moon's bitter smile and the hard way he spoke the word *jail* told him his brother had changed. But his heart ached at finding Moon, only to lose him again.

His feelings must have shown because Moon gave him a quick grin and said, 'Don't suppose you'd stay with me, Sam? Turn sea pirate?'

Sam shook his head. 'Someone's got to go back and tell Ma you're alive! Anyway, I'd be a really bad sea pirate. I get seasick.'

Moon threw back his head and laughed, his old open, friendly laugh. 'Land pirate, sea pirate, you're still my brother. Whatever we do, wherever we go, however many seas lie between us. Blood's thicker than water, Sam – even saltwater. You hold on to that knife and remember: *We are kings of the forest, let them tame us if they can.*'

'It's beautifully made. Ebony, inlaid with mother of pearl.' Sparrow admired the knife's handle. 'Where did you get it?'

'That would be telling.' Moon winked. 'Sam, get some rest. Us folks will be parleying into the night.'

Thirty-three

S am woke later to find someone had wrapped him in a blanket. Beside the dying embers of the fire, Sparrow and Jay were still talking to Moon. As far as he could tell from the low murmur of voices, their talk was friendly enough – the main disagreement seemed to be about the Collector.

The Collector! Sam remembered he was down in a part of the cave the pirates called the hole – still imprisoned and unaware of what was going on. He listened more carefully.

Sparrow wanted to take him back to the mainland in the *Dugong*. But Moon flatly refused to give his captive up.

'You got to understand – it's a question of reputation. I'm the Jalai Rajah!'

'Look, Mr Singh – if I had the ransom money now, I'd give it to you myself!' Sparrow told him. 'You can't keep the professor for ever – he's not a young man. And I don't hold out hope of the governor raising that much money.'

'Call me Moon, Princess. Now listen, I'm grateful to you, looking out for Sam and offering him safe passage home. But I can't let old blabbermouth go without a ransom – much as I'd like to be rid of him. If I do, they'll say the Jalai Rajah's gone soft!'

'*Sam Singh! Lola!*' Sam sat up, hearing his name and called out happily, 'Suka – where are you, boy?'

In a flurry of green, the parrot swooped to circle the lagoon and swept out again, still squawking.

'Suka?' Sam whistled. 'Come back!'

The others had stopped talking.

'You didn't go and bring that bird over the high seas?' Moon shook his head.

'I did,' Sam told him. 'And he's taught the other parrots on the Isle how to speak. But why did he say Lola? She's back at the village—'

A wooden spear shot swiftly over their heads, brushing Moon's hair and impaling itself with a twang in the far wall.

'*What the*—' Moon turned to look over his shoulder at the spear, now embedded in the limestone. 'A few centimetres lower and that would have blinded me left eye!'

'Stand up and raise your hands, pirate! Or the next one's going straight into you!'

Moon stood up slowly. Sam did too. That voice was familiar.

'Hands on your head!' it called. 'Sam, I'll watch him while you come to us.'

'*Lola!* Don't worry—' Sam broke into a run. He hadn't known her in the strange echoing cave.

'Sam? Are you really all right?' Lola took a hesitant step towards him, Suka perched on her shoulder. Tuke and the Johns, armed with spears and a machete, edged into the firelight.

Sam greeted Tuke first, then the two Johns. He bumped foreheads with Lola and took Suka on to his own shoulder.

'Lola! I'm so happy to see you. What are you doing here?'

Lola rolled her eyes. 'I came to rescue you from the pirates, of course! I didn't know you'd got all *matey* with them – what's going on?'

Lola had spotted the Jalai Rajah's flag and watched from the clifftop as the pirates hooked Sam's canoe in. She'd run back to the village to fetch the others, then rowed with the Johns to the cave, guided by Suka, and waited until the dead of night to ambush the pirates and free Sam.

'Brother – have you made friends with every single person on this Isle?' They turned to see Moon staring in astonishment, hands still on his head.

'Sam does have a way with him, by the Lady!' Sparrow came over to greet Tuke and the Johns. She went to give Lola a hug, but the girl raised a hand.

'Wait – what did that pirate say? *Brother?*'

More explanations followed, Tuke retrieved his spear amid laughter and Moon offered to make everyone tea.

'How did you manage to sneak past the pirate ship?' Jay asked.

Tuke laughed and explained. 'We're very quiet,' Lola translated for him.

'And the crew will be out cold by now. Mad for grog, that lot!' Moon added. He crouched by a small stove, boiling water. 'Me, I don't touch the stuff. Cold tea in an old Bengal Rum bottle – that's how I keep them fooled!'

'I'm glad to see you, Lola,' Sparrow told her.

Tuke spoke. 'My grandfather thanks you for picking me up in the *Dugong*,' Lola translated.

'But what were you all saying about the Collector? Voices echo a long way in these caves, you know.'

Moon brought them tea on a silver tray. 'It's like this, Miss Lola. I don't want to keep the professor here – he's driving us barmy with all his talk. But I'm the Jalai Rajah, deadliest pirate in the Kalinga Sea!' He poured steaming liquid from a blue-patterned china teapot into matching cups. 'Got me fearsome reputation to think of, haven't I?'

'Fearsome?' Sparrow looked pointedly at the tea service and raised her eyebrows.

'Good honest pirate plunder, this!' he told her. 'Finest porcelain all the way from China – took it off a ship bound for the governor's own table. If he hears I let the professor go, those folks will soon be swarming this part of the Isle!'

'That's true!' Lola agreed. 'The Jalai Rajah and his men do a good job keeping strangers from the north. And anyway, what about the *people*? The ones whose skulls the Collector stole?'

'Skulls – what does he want with skulls?' Moon frowned.

They explained, while the fire was stoked, more talk flowed, and they drank another round of tea. Through it all, Sam's mind was working. He had the glimmer of an idea, faint as the fleeting sparks from the fire.

'Let's decide what everyone wants,' he began. 'Lola, your people want strangers kept from this part of the Isle.' He turned to Jay and Sparrow. 'Jay – you need a ship to take you where you can live as a free man—'

'And work for Indica!' Jay interrupted. 'I have a comrade in Singapura who'd take me in.'

Sam nodded at his brother. 'Moon and his crew want to get rid of the Collector,' he went on. 'But they need a ransom – to keep their status as dreaded pirates.'

'I'd pay if I had the money on me,' Sparrow put in. 'Now Jay's out, all I want is to go home to Moonlally. Ophelia and Shri feel the same way.'

'I think I might have a plan.' Sam looked round at the expectant faces, softly lit by warm firelight.

Lola clapped her hands. 'Sam *Singh*! I knew you'd thought of something – I could tell from your expression. Go on, then – spill it.'

Sam looked at Moon. 'Brother, suppose you take Jay to Singapura on your pirate ship? In exchange, we'll take the Collector back to the mainland.'

'Trade captives?' Moon mused. 'Not against the idea. But where's the money for Jay's ransom coming from?'

'Once I'm home, I'll wire money to Jay's friend in Singapura to pay you! Fifty gold pieces, same as the professor's ransom. Your reputation will remain intact,' Sparrow promised.

'Which means strangers will stay away from the north of the Isle,' Lola added.

'I can navigate the ship to Singapura – that's what I'm trained for,' Jay told them.

'But wait.' Lola held her hands up. 'What about the people he stole? I *saw* those people, Sam. Everything was taken from them and the Collector thought it was all right to steal their remains. How do we show him that's wrong?'

Sparrow shook her head. 'I'm not sure you can teach people like him, Lola. They must learn on their own. Besides, he's been a captive here. I'd say he's had his punishment.'

Moon cleared his throat. 'I got two things to say. First to Miss Lola. When we captured that professor, he wouldn't stop scribbling pirate speak in his notebook. So, we took it off him. Now you've told me about his cracked ideas, I don't think he deserves it back, is what I'm saying. Bogusz by name, *bogus* by nature, if you ask me.'

'That seems fair,' Jay answered. 'And the second thing?'

'Second is to all of you. We're going to need your help. If the *Sea Demon*'s sailing to Singapura, that leaky old tub's going to need work to make her seaworthy. Singapura's a good 800 kilometres!'

Sam looked at the others. 'Well?'

Sparrow smiled at him. 'Of course we'll help! The *Dugong*'s captain is the finest inventor in all Indica!'

'And the two Johns build the best canoes on the Isle!' Lola added. She turned to translate for the Johns, who nodded in agreement. 'We'll help you fix the *Sea Demon*,' she told Moon seriously. 'Sam Singh's saved my life twice now. If he thinks this is a plan – well, then, it is.'

Thirty-four

When Sam Singh was older and he looked back at his life – all this came much later – he knew he owed everything to his time on the Isle. By then, he was known for being a good leader and a good man, qualities that are rarely found in a person.

He learned many important truths on the Isle: that the dead are never really gone and the living are always in their debt. He learned that the earth does not belong to us, but like all living creatures, we belong to the earth. He learned this from Lola and Tuke, and now, repairing the *Sea Demon*, he learned that however different people might seem, they could work together for what really mattered.

At the time, Sam did not realise any of this. But he did know, for the days it took to prepare the pirate ship for its voyage, that he was as happy as he had ever been. The *Sea Demon* was dragged up on to the beach, the *Dugong* anchored in open sea beyond the lagoon. He and Lola paddled back and forth in one of the lifeboats, hauling bamboo for sail battens or heaving padauk trunks from the forests with the Johns. A small crew was kept aboard the submersible, and Sam, with Suka on his shoulder, often took over from Shri in the *Dugong*.

Sparrow decided she would be most useful as cook, and sent a disgruntled Moon off for supplies.

'Just so long as that princess don't tell no one about this!' he'd say to Sam and Lola as he returned with a net of crabs or a sea turtle from the lagoon. 'Can't have folks thinking the Jalai Rajah sits about fishing!' Moon cheered up when he was sent hunting with the Johns, returning with a huge wild pig that fed them all for a week. He was told never to hunt the dugongs, whom they often saw in the mangrove swamps on their way into the forest. The animals would chirp out a friendly chorus and swim alongside their boat, poking smiling snouts out to greet them.

'When Tuke sent the dugongs to rescue you,' began Sam, trying to understand what had happened that night, 'how did he do it? Does Tuke speak their language?'

Lola scrunched her face up. 'Sort of. There's more to it than that. Tuke knows how to become part of their world. He can look at the seabed with the dugong herd or see the Isle from above like the parrots!' She pointed up at Suka, circling the skies with his raucous flock.

'That's amazing! Will you be able to do that, one day?'

Lola shrugged. 'It's going to take hard work. But this has been fun, Sam Singh. I'm glad we could repair the *Sea Demon* together!'

Sam smiled at her. 'I never thanked you properly. For coming to save me.'

'Well, I'm pleased you found your brother. Even if he *is* a pirate.'

To Sam's surprise, the pirates set to and did the work of repairing the ship without protest. They hacked the padauk into planks, which Shri taught them to dovetail into position, and caulked seams with hemp rope, sealed with resin from the island's trees.

Soon the *Sea Demon* was a different ship from the one that had snared Sam. Her dark timbers gleamed, the square tanja sails had been lime-washed and neatly patched. Every part of her was sound enough for a long sea voyage. To Moon's annoyance, Ophelia had even given the Jalai Rajah's scarlet skull-and-crossbones a proper wash.

'It was filthy and disgusting!' she told him.

'It's *meant* to be filthy and disgusting – how else is it going to strike fear into men's hearts?' Moon growled back. But everyone knew he didn't mean it.

'The *Sea Demon*'s a new ship, brother,' Sam told him, as they sat on the beach roasting mackerel over the fire.

Moon narrowed his eyes at the boat, still beached on her side, sails furled. 'Is it though? Got a question for you, Sam. If all the planks on deck have been replaced, every seam's caulked fresh and the rigging's new, is the *Sea Demon* the same ship?'

Sam thought about this as he flipped his fish over. The *Sea Demon* was still the *Sea Demon* – not just because it had the same name, but because the *idea* of the ship was what mattered. To the pirates it was their home and their livelihood, their mother and father. You could almost say they loved it.

'Yes,' he decided.

'Good answer.' His brother spat out a fishbone. 'Ships are always being made new. Just like people. Sometimes it's hard to recognise them when they've changed. But their old self is in there. Even if you don't see it at first.'

Sam nodded. He thought of how Tuke had found Moon's spirit, dim from his time in jail, and realised what his brother meant.

'I lost meself for a while, Sam. But seeing you come all this way for *me*, I remember who I once was. That's why I've decided to change her name,' Moon nodded towards the ship.

'The *Sea Demon*? Why?'

'Reasons. Your Miss Ophelia painted the new name in gold today. They said she has the neatest hand.'

'What are you changing it to?'

'I wanted to surprise you when we launch. But I'll be on me ship and I won't know what you think of it down the end of a telescope. *Samudra Raksa* is her new name. Come on – let's take a look.'

'Samudra? Like my name – Samudra Singh?' He scrambled up to follow his brother.

'Exactly. Your name means sea or ocean, same as that great city you was named after. And Raksa means demon – but it can also mean guardian. So, she's the *Sea Demon* – and the *Sea Guardian*.'

'Because she guards the Isle for Lola and her people.'

'Exactly. You always were a smart one, little brother.' Moon scuffed at the sand as they walked down the beach. 'Sam – I know I don't write too good, but if I send you the odd note through the princess...'

'I can pick your letters up from Moonlally!'

That was something, he supposed. Lola had promised to write and so had his brother. It didn't make it any less painful, but from now on, visiting Moonlally would mean letters from those he'd left behind.

'Here she is – shipshape, if I say so meself!'

And there it was. Her new name, *Samudra Raksa*, painted in looping gold letters on the port side of the bow. Sam swallowed. It meant everything to know that wherever his brother sailed, out on the vast and endless sea, his own name would travel with him.

Moon slapped him on the back. 'Fair wind tomorrow and a new moon – handsome weather for us sea pirates,' he told him. 'Look smart, Sam. Time you learned to hoist the rigging. The *Samudra Raksa* is ready to set sail.'

Thirty-five

At high tide the following morning, it took twenty pirates to haul the *Samudra Raksa* out to sea. Lola and Sam were on board, hoisting the square sails and watching the wind curve them out, full-bellied. The deck slanted under their feet and the ship tugged restlessly at her anchor, eager to be off.

Beyond the bay, Sam could see the *Dugong,* rays of sun glinting off her metal skin. He looked down at the boats tethered to the *Samudra Raksa.* One was a dugout canoe, waiting to take Lola back to the Isle. The other was the *Dugong*'s lifeboat, for him to join the crew on the submersible.

Sam's heart sank a little further at the thought of another journey with the Collector. How would he put up with him?

While they'd readied the pirate ship for its long voyage, the man had remained in the cave below. Sam tried to persuade Moon to unshackle him, but Moon insisted. The Collector had to believe the pirates were deadly cut-throats, and he'd escaped with his life, or their plan would fail. It had been distressing to see him confined – however badly the Collector behaved, Sam did not think anyone deserved to lose their freedom. It didn't help that he disliked him – in fact, it made him feel worse.

That morning, Sam had gone with Sparrow – in her manservant's turban – to tell the captive he was free to travel with the princess to the mainland. The Collector had not been happy at this news.

'Outrageous! I have valuable specimens at the Residence. I demand your princess take me to the port in her seacraft. Immediately!'

Sparrow folded her arms. 'The princess has paid your ransom and is escorting you to the mainland. Just as the governor ordered.'

'I don't believe the governor would agree to such a thing!'

Sam was about to speak, but Sparrow shot him a glance and gave a slight shake of her head. 'I hear a complaint has been made about your research methods. Ancestral remains were stolen from Lola's grandfather's hut. The governor is *furious*.'

'Nonsense!' the Collector spluttered. 'I never touched the skull. Besides – you can't prove anything!'

Sparrow raised an eyebrow. 'I didn't mention the word *skull*. I'd watch what you say until you're off the Isle,' she told him. 'You have a choice: return with us or remain at the mercy of the pirates.'

The Collector nodded, deflated.

'Better get this off, then, hadn't we?' Sparrow kneeled to saw through the Collector's leg shackle with a metal cutter. 'The pirate ship's waiting in the bay,' she warned. 'The Jalai Rajah's holding fire while you board the *Dugong*. If I were you, I'd behave until we're clear of his waters.'

'And the notebook? My research?'

Sparrow shrugged. 'Probably at the bottom of the lagoon,' she told him.

The Collector's notebook was in fact burning a hole in Sam's pocket. He'd asked Lola whether she wanted the part where the Collector had written down her people's language.

'No, thanks! Most of it was rubbish, anyway – I made it up. As if we would give our words to *him*. Words have power. That's why the Johns are the Johns. They don't tell strangers their real names.'

'But what about your name? And Tuke?'

'Lola? That's the name the governor gave me, not my *real* name. That's private. And Tuke's more of a –' she scrunched up her face, thinking – '*title*. Like the governor.' She glanced at Sam, her dark eyes narrowing. 'Sam – I think I might be ready to tell you my real name.' And she leaned forward to murmur it quickly in his ear, her soft hair brushing his cheek.

Now the moment had come. He watched Lola settle at the prow, giving him a wave as she began to row the canoe through rolling sea towards the shore. Sam waved back, whispering her name under his breath.

It was time. He shook Jay's hand and gave his brother a final hug, his heart heavy.

'Cheer up, Sam. This ain't goodbye but – what they call it? *Au revoir*,' Moon told him. 'I've asked the princess to give you my share of the ransom. When you get home, find Ma and give it her directly. Don't let that new fella get his hands on it.'

'I will. But I'll miss you, brother.' His eyes watered – the salt in the sea wind, he told himself. *Au revoir* meant *until we meet again*. When?

'*Goodbye, namaste, poitu vaaren, au revoir!*' Suka shrieked, circling overhead.

'I mean it, Sam,' Moon assured him. 'Jay says Indica's going to be free one day!' He slapped him on the shoulder. 'Once you see Ma, my advice is head back to Moonlally and the princess. With any luck, I'll visit you in the palace someday!'

Sam shot him a wry smile. He didn't know where he'd go after giving his mother the money. But he did know that a land pirate's life, though honourable in its own way, wasn't for him. He wanted to help his people – like Lola. And to do that, he'd have to leave them for a while.

Thirty-six

It took no time for Sam to clamber into the lifeboat, row out and board the *Dugong*. The vessel plunged beneath the water in a loud chorus of cheeps. As they descended, Sam watched the wild dugongs roving overhead: two full-grown and a baby, who bumped its smiling face curiously against the glass. Sam smiled back.

Out on the open sea, the *Samudra Raksa* was slicing through the water, red flag lowered, for as Moon had explained to Sam, the skull-and-crossbones was raised only when a target was in sight, meaning no quarter would be given to those on board.

'We're not planning on doing any pirating this voyage. Need to get Jay safely to Singapura.' He'd paused. 'Unless we see a ship too full of booty to let pass. Then I'll have to raise the *Samudra Raksa*'s red flag. Rude not to.'

Once a pirate, always a pirate. Moon had been a land pirate, now he was king of the sea. But that didn't have to be true for everyone.

Back on the Isle, with its black cliffs and jade-green forests, Lola, Tuke and the Johns were making their way to the village, where Lola would train with her grandfather to become their shaman. Suka was flying somewhere in the blue above but Sam knew he would swoop down to see him next time they breached.

The Collector had been supplied with ink, pen, paper and a wooden writing slope, and was scribbling away. Ophelia was checking the medical equipment on board. Sam made for the cockpit, where Sparrow and Shri were busy. He stood back, watching the hum of activity.

'Cruising speed set! Due to surface again in twenty.' Sparrow leaned forward to adjust the controls. She was acting as first mate and would pilot the submarine alongside Shri, taking shifts and napping in the cockpit.

Shri nodded to Sam. 'You can be second mate. This boy's quick,' he told Sparrow. 'Got the hang of the *Dugong* completely. We might let him pilot some of the way.'

'Yes, please!' Sam hoped to stay in the cockpit, avoiding the Collector as much as possible.

Sparrow smiled at him. 'Would you like to learn more about this sort of thing, Sam? Shri has an engineering school back in Moonlally. They invent all sorts of mechanical wonders.'

This sounded marvellous to Sam, and quite different from the schools he was used to. But a school like that would cost money. And he didn't have a silver anna to his name. The Collector hadn't paid him, and the money Sparrow would give him – Moon's share of the ransom – was for Ma.

'It helps, you know,' Sparrow told him. 'When you miss someone badly, it helps to concentrate on stuff that's very hard to learn. And don't worry about money. Shri's school is free – with boarding too!'

'But I haven't done much schooling,' he told her. 'I might not be clever enough.'

'Nonsense. You've got aptitude and the drive to learn. I've noticed it myself!'

'We'd be happy to have you, Sam,' Shri put in.

'Could I do that?' Sam's heart lifted. He felt happiness buoy him, like the *Dugong* surfacing from the cool blue depths towards warm sunlight.

Ophelia poked her head around the cockpit door. 'Chaps – I need Sam. The professor's driving me loopy!' she hissed. 'Please come and talk to him. I've got work to do.'

Sam followed her into the cabin. The Collector waved his pen when he came in. 'Right. Good that you're here, boy. I want you to read out what I've written, slowly and clearly.' He handed Sam a sheaf of papers and lay back on his bunk.

Sam cleared his throat. '*The True Adventures of Professor B on a Tropical Isle, Involving Encounters with Savages, Pirates and a Daring Escape with a Princess,*' he read. Ophelia gave a muffled gasp of laughter and the Collector frowned at her.

Sam began to read the story aloud. He was not pleased to find himself featured as a loyal servant boy, Sammy, complete with tame parrot. And the Collector's version of events sounded very different from what he recalled.

'*"Please, sir, what is that monstrous black building?" little Sammy asked.*

"Why, lad, 'tis the deadly Octopus, where traitors are locked away. This Isle may look a paradise but 'tis tragically infested with savages and its shores are hotbeds of dread pirates. Stick with me, Sammy, and you need not fear."

"I will, kind sir." The lad smiled gratefully up at his benefactor.'

After a few minutes more, Sam was relieved when the Collector closed his eyes and began to snore.

'Thank goodness!' Ophelia called. 'Not surprised he sent himself to sleep. What utter rubbish.'

Sam set down the Collector's pages, picked up a blank sheet and looked at it. He wasn't a good writer, but he'd have to practise. For a start, he wanted to write Lola a long letter.

And he needed to set things right. Sam had flicked through the pages of the Collector's notebook and found a list of numbers – the record of the skulls the Collector had taken. Beside each number was the name of the tribe and the part of the world where they lived. Sam intended to find their addresses and write, explaining what had happened to their kin. He owed them that much.

As for the Collector, Sam realised he no longer owed him anything. The Collector had brought him to the Isle but Sam had bargained for – and won – the man's freedom in return. They were even.

Sparrow came into the cabin. 'The *Dugong*'s ready to breach if you want to help?' She glanced at the Collector's title page and snorted. 'Is there no end to that man's foolishness? You ought to write down what *really* happened, Sam!'

Sam followed her, wondering. Could he do that? Tell of his adventures on the Isle of Lost Voices – so different from the Collector's?

Sam settled into the co-pilot's seat and slowly pulled the ballast lever. As the submarine ascended towards the bright, rippling surface, he decided to try. One day, when he'd practised enough, he would write his own account of what had happened on the Isle. *Words have power*, Lola had told him, and maybe she was right. He'd tell the truth as he remembered it and when he did, he knew exactly what to call his story.

He'd call it: *The Voyage of Sam Singh.*

About the Author

Gita Ralleigh is a medical doctor who studied for an MA in Creative Writing and has published short stories and two poetry collections. Her debut novel *The Destiny of Minou Moonshine* was longlisted for the Branford Boase Award 2024. Gita lives in London with her two children, and teaches creative writing at Imperial College.

About the Author

Acknowledgements

I had the absolute joy and privilege of using the London Library's wonderful collection and building while drafting *The Voyage of Sam Singh;* thank you to talented Emerging Writers: Fatima Cham, Gayathiri Kamalakanthan, Kimberley Sheehan and Sarah Stribley for reading Sam's adventures at an early stage! Much gratitude to London Shah also for her perceptive feedback.

I'm completely humbled that many established authors have generously championed my debut *The Destiny of Minou Moonshine*, especially former teachers Anthony McGowan and Michael Rosen and the incomparably kind and encouraging Sita Brahmachari.

I owe so much to the Faberites: Allison DeFrees, Faye Bird, Barbara Rustin, Beverley D'Silva, Michelle Wood and Maria Waldron.

Special thanks to Janet Noble for arranging my first ever school visit!

My fellow Kinara poets are an invaluable support: Anita Pati, Sarala Estruch, Rushika Wick, Sylee Gore and extra thanks to Shash Trevett for help with Suka's Tamil vocabulary!

I am incredibly grateful to my lovely agent Catherine Pellegrino and exceptional editor Lauren Atherton for all their hard work, also Fiona Kennedy and her team at Zephyr/Head of Zeus and copyeditor Jenny Glencross. A huge thanks to Polly Grice at Head of Zeus and Sabina Maharjan at EDPR for their help with launching this book into the world. Thank you to Weitong Mai and Jessie Price for the gorgeous cover.

All love and gratitude to my beautiful family, I am unbelievably lucky to have you.

Finally, I would like to acknowledge all the amazing teachers, librarians, teaching assistants and volunteers I have met in schools, who work tirelessly to ensure every child has access to the magic of reading.

Author note

The inspiration for this book comes from real Indian history recorded in 19th and 20th century colonial texts. The Isle of Lost Voices is based on the Andaman Islands in the Indian Ocean, now part of India. These tropical islands were used by the British as a penal colony for prisoners from the subcontinent and housed a notorious jail. The Andamans appear most famously in Arthur Conan Doyle's *The Sign of Four*, still on the GCSE syllabus today.

Sam's people were described in a book published in 1928 called *The Land Pirates of India* which dismissed his nomadic tribe as 'hereditary criminals'. The world of Lola, Sam's friend and ally, comes from writings about the Andamans' indigenous population, particularly the Jarawa. As outsiders, Sam and Lola develop a close bond and share a deep sense of injustice and unfairness.

Many young readers I meet, like my own children, see themselves as both Indian and British. Sometimes the weight of the shared histories they inherit can seem difficult to explain, let alone turn into fiction. The real stories of children like Sam and Lola were not recorded in their own words, so imagination is needed to fill history's empty spaces and shine light upon those in the shadows. Sam's voyage to the Isle in search of his brother reframes history through his eyes; he discovers words have power, and that he can use their power to tell his own story.

Gita Ralleigh
London, 2024